The Doll

Also by Daphne du Maurier

Fiction

The Loving Spirit
I'll Never Be Young Again
Julius
Jamaica Inn
Rebecca
Frenchman's Creek
Hungry Hill
The King's General
The Parasites
My Cousin Rachel
The Birds and Other Stories
The Scapegoat
The Breaking Point: Short Stories
Castle Dor (with Sir Arthur Quiller-Couch)
The Flight of the Falcon
The House on the Strand
Don't Look Now
Rule Britannia
The Rendezvous and Other Stories

Nonfiction

Gerald: A Portrait
The Du Mauriers
Mary Anne
The Infernal World of Branwell Brontë
The Glass-Blowers
Vanishing Cornwall
Golden Lads: A Story of Anthony Bacon, Francis, and Their Friends
The Winding Stair: Francis Bacon, His Rise and Fall
Myself When Young: The Shaping of a Writer
The Rebecca *Notebook and Other Memories*
Enchanted Cornwall

The Doll

THE LOST SHORT STORIES

Daphne du Maurier

HARPER

NEW YORK · LONDON · TORONTO · SYDNEY

HARPER

THE DOLL. Copyright © 2011 by Chichester Partnership. All rights reserved. Printed in the United States of America. No part of this book may be used or reproduced in any manner whatsoever without written permission except in the case of brief quotations embodied in critical articles and reviews. For information address HarperCollins Publishers, 10 East 53rd Street, New York, NY 10022.

"And Now to God the Father" first published in Great Britain in *The Bystander*, May 1929.

"A Difference in Temperament" first published in Great Britain in *The Bystander*, June 1929.

"And His Letters Grew Colder" first published in the USA in *Hearst's International Combined with Cosmopolitan,* September 1931.

"The Happy Valley" first published in Great Britain in the *Illustrated London News*, 1932.

"The Doll" from *The Editor Regrets*, edited by George Joseph, published in Great Britain by Michael Joseph in 1937.

"Frustration," "Tame Cat," "Mazie," "Nothing Hurts for Long," and "Week-End" from *Early Stories*, published in Great Britain by Todd in 1955.

"The Limpet" from *The Breaking Point*, published in the USA by Doubleday and Co. in 1959.

"East Wind" from *the Rebecca Notebook*, published in the USA by Doubleday and Co. in 1980.

An edition of this collection was printed in Great Britain in 2011 by Virago Press.

ISBN 978-1-61793-498-8

Acknowledgments

The estate of Daphne du Maurier would like to thank
Ann Willmore for her help in rediscovering some of
the stories in this collection.

Contents

The Doll

East Wind

Nearly a hundred miles west of the Scillies, far
from the main track of ships, lies the small, rocky
island of St Hilda's. Only a few miles square, it
is a barren, rugged place, with great jagged cliffs that run
steep into deep water. The harbour is hardly more than a
creek, and the entrance like a black hole cut out of the
rock. The island rises out of the sea a queer, misshapen
crag, splendid in its desolation, with a grey face lifted to
the four winds. It might have been thrown up from the
depths of the Atlantic in a moment of great unrest, and
set there, a small defiant piece of land, to withstand forever
the anger of the sea. Over a century ago few knew of its
existence, and the many sailors who saw its black outline
on the horizon imagined it to be little more than a solitary
rock, standing like a sentinel in mid-ocean.

The population of St Hilda's has never exceeded
seventy, and the people are descendants of the original
settlers from the Scillies and Western Ireland. Their
only means of livelihood used to be the catching of fish
and the cultivation of the soil. Today things are greatly
changed, owing to the monthly call of a coastal steamer,
and the installation of wireless. But in the middle half
of the last century, years would sometimes pass without
communication with the mainland, and the people had
degenerated into quiet, listless folk, the inevitable result

of intermarriage. There were no books then, no papers, and even the small chapel that had been built by the original settlers had fallen into disuse. Year in, year out, the life remained unchanged, with never a new face or a fresh thought to break the monotony of the days. Sometimes, on the horizon, the faint glimmer of a sail would be seen, and the people would gaze with wonder in their eyes, but slowly the sail would become a far-off speck, and the unknown ship pass into oblivion.

They were peaceable folk, these natives of St Hilda's, born to a quiet, untroubled existence as monotonous as the waves that broke against their shores. They knew nothing of the world beyond the island, they saw no more momentous happenings than birth and death and the changes of the seasons. Their lives were untouched by great emotions, by great sorrows; their desires had never been lit, but lay imprisoned within their souls. They lived blindly, happily, like children, content to grope in the dark and never to search for the something that lay beyond their darkness. Some inner sense warned them that in their ignorance dwelt security, a happiness that was never wild, never triumphant, but peaceful and silent. They walked with their eyes to the ground; they had become weary of looking upon a sea where no ship came, of lifting their faces to a sky that seldom changed.

Summer and winter passed, children grew into men and women – there was no more in life than these things. Far away lay the other lands dwelt in by strange people, where the life was said to be hard and men had to fight for their existence. Sometimes an islander would sail away, shaping his course for the mainland and promising to return with news of the rest of the world. Perhaps he was drowned, or picked up by some passing ship; no one could say, for he never came back. No one who left the island returned. Even the few ships that so rarely visited St Hilda's came once only, and passed not again.

It was almost as if there were no such place, as if the island were a dream, a phantom creation of a sailor's brain, something rising out of the sea at midnight as a challenge to reality, then vanishing in surf and mist to be forgotten, to be half-consciously remembered years later, flickering for a bewildered second in a dusty brain as a dead thought. Yet to the people of St Hilda's the island was reality, the ships that came and went were their phantoms.

There was only the island. Beyond it lay the ghostly, the intangible; the truth was in the seared rock, in the touch of the soil, in the sound of the waves breaking against the cliffs. This was the belief of the humble fisherfolk, and they cast their nets during the day, and gossiped over the harbour wall at evening with never a thought of the lands across the sea. At dawn the men set off to fish, and when their nets were filled they would return to the island and climb the steep path that led to the fields, to work with stolid patience at the soil.

The group of cottages was clustered together at the water's edge, with seldom more than two rooms to contain an entire family. Here the women bent over their fires, cooked, and darned their men's clothes, talking peacefully from dawn till dusk.

One cottage stood apart from the others, built high on the cliff and looking down upon the creek. Today only the site remains, and instead of a cottage stands the ugly wireless station; but sixty years ago this was the home of the chief fisherman of St Hilda's. Here Guthrie dwelt with his wife

Jane, living as children, content in each other, unmindful of desire, ignorant of distress.

Guthrie stood on the cliffs at twilight, watching the sea. Below him in the harbour the fishing boats rocked, moored for the night. The men gossiped over the harbour wall and the sound of their voices rose to him, mingled with the thin cries of children. The little quay was slippery with spray and blood and the scales of dead fish. The smoke curled from the chimneys, a thin blue column, twisting and turning in the air. From the door of his cottage came Jane, her hands to her eyes, searching for him. 'Come away down!' she called. 'The supper's been ready an hour since. Ye'll find un spoilt, as likely as not.' He waved his arm and turned, pausing to glance at the horizon for the last time. The sky was speckled with white loose-flocked clouds, and the sea, changing from the oily smoothness of the day, was running past the harbour in a low swell. Already there was a wash upon the rocks, at the eastward entrance. A soft humming sound came to his ears, as the sea gathered force, and a cool breeze played with his hair. He ran down the hill to the village, and cried to the fishermen who were standing by the wall.

''Tis the East Wind startin',' he told them. 'Can't ye see the sky like a fish's tail, and the big lumpin' sea awash on the rocks? Before midnight there'll be a gale to blow your heads off, and the sea angrier than the devil himself. Look to the boats.'

The harbour was sheltered from the wind, yet the vessels were moored securely fore and aft to prevent the possibility of their breaking adrift.

After he had seen that everything was safe for the night, Guthrie climbed the path to his cottage on the cliff. He ate his supper in silence. He felt restless and excited; the quiet atmosphere of the cottage seemed to oppress him. He tried to occupy himself in mending a hole in one of his nets, but he could not give his mind to the task. The net slipped from his hands; he turned his head and listened. It seemed as if a cry had risen out of the night. Yet there was nothing, only the low hum of the wind, and the sound of surf breaking upon the rocks. He sighed and gazed into the fire, oddly disturbed, his soul heavy within him.

In the bedroom, with her head by the window, Jane knelt, listening to the sea. Her heart beat strangely, her hands trembled, she wanted to creep from the cottage and run onto the cliffs where she would feel the true force of the wind. It would strike upon her breast and sweep the hair from her face, she would hear the singing of it in her ears, she would smell the salt tang of the spray as it stung her lips and her eyes. The longing came upon her to laugh with the wind, to cry with the sea, to open wide her arms and be possessed by something which would envelop her like a dark cloak and prevent her from straying far away on the lonely cliffs amongst the tall grass. She prayed for the day to dawn, not gently as was its custom, but fiercely, with the sun burning the fields and the wind sweeping the white-edged seas, bringing destruction. She would stand and wait upon the shore, feeling the wet sand beneath her naked feet.

A footstep sounded outside the room and she turned with a little shiver from the window. It was Guthrie. He gazed at her solemnly and bade her shut out the sound of the wind. They undressed quietly and lay beside each other in the narrow bed without a word. He could feel the warmth of her body, but his heart was not with her. His thoughts left his form, imprisoned there at her side,

5

and fled into the night. She felt him go, yet minded not. She put away his cold hands from her, and gave herself to her own dreams, where he could have no entrance.

Thus they slept together in each other's arms, yet separately; like dead things in a grave, their souls long vanished and forgotten.

When they awoke the dawn had broken in the sky. The sun shone blindly from a blue heaven, scorching the earth. Great seas, tipped with foam, crashed against the cliff and swept the rocks outside the harbour, and all the while the East Wind blew, tossing the grass, scattering the hot white sand, forcing its triumphant path through the white mist and the green waves like a demon let loose upon the island.

Guthrie went to the window and looked out upon the day. A cry came from his lips and he ran from the cottage, unable to believe his eyes. Jane followed him. The folk in the other cottages had risen too and stood staring at the harbour, their hands lifted in amazement, their excited voices filling the air with sound yet fading away, indistinguishable from the wind. For there in the harbour, dwarfing the little fishing boats with her great spars, the sails stretched upon her yards to dry in the morning sun, lay a brig at anchor, rocking against wind and tide.

Guthrie stood on the quay amongst the crowd of fishermen. The whole of St Hilda's was gathered there to welcome the strangers from the brig. Tall, dark men they were, these sailors from beyond the sea, with narrow almond eyes and white teeth that gleamed as they laughed. They spoke in a different tongue. Guthrie and his fellows questioned them, while the women and children surrounded them with

6

gaping mouths, gazing into their faces, feeling their clothes with timid, wondering hands.

'How did ye find the entrance to the harbour,' cried Guthrie, 'with the wind an' the sea in league together against ye? 'Tis the devil himself that hath sent ye here maybe.'

The sailors laughed and shook their heads. They could not understand what he said. Their eyes wandered beyond him and the fishermen to the women. They smiled and spoke amongst themselves, happy at their discovery.

All the while the sun beat down upon their heads and the East Wind blew, scorching the air like a breath from hell. No man went forth to fish that day. Great mountainous seas thundered past the harbour mouth and the fishing boats remained at anchor, small and insignificant beside the strange brig.

Something of madness seemed to fall upon the people of St Hilda's. Their nets lay neglected and unmended beside their cottage doors, the fields and flowers remained untended on the hills above the village. There was no interest in their lives but the sailors from the ship. They clambered upon the brig, leaving no part of her unvisited, they touched the strangers' clothes with excited, inquisitive fingers. The sailors laughed at them, they hunted in the sea chests and gave the men cigarettes, they found bright scarves and coloured kerchiefs for the women. Guthrie led them out upon the cliffs, swaggering a little like a young boy, a cigarette between his lips.

The fishermen threw wide their cottage doors, jealous of one another's hospitality, each one desirous of extending the greatest welcome. The sailors soon explored the island; they thought it a poor, barren place, without interest. They descended to the shore and formed themselves into groups on the quayside, yawning, idle, hoping for a change of weather. The time hung heavily upon their hands.

Still the East Wind blew, scattering the sand, turning the earth to dust. The sun blazed from a cloudless sky, the big seas swept round the shores, green, foam-flecked, twisting and turning like a live thing. The sun set streaky and windswept, pointing orange fingers to the sky. The night came, warm and alive. The very air was restless. The sailors found the disused chapel at the end of the village and encamped there, fetching tobacco and brandy from the brig.

There seemed to be no order amongst them. They had no discipline, they obeyed no rules. Two men only remained on the brig to watch. The fisherfolk wondered not at their conduct; their presence on the island was so wonderful and rare a thing, nothing counted but this. They joined the sailors in the chapel, they tasted brandy for the first time. The night rang with cries and song. The island was a new place now, broken of peace, swayed by suggestion and filled with strange desires. Guthrie stood amongst his companions, his cheeks flushed, his cold eyes bright and foolish. He held a glass in his hand, he swallowed the brandy with deep, contented draughts. He laughed with the sailors, wildly, without reason; what did it matter if he could not understand their words? The lights swayed before his eyes, the ground sloped beneath his feet, it seemed as if he had never lived before. The wind could shout and the sea thunder and roar, the world called to him now. Beyond the island lay the other lands, the homes of these sailors. Here he would find life, and beauty, and strange, incredible adventures. No more would he bend his back, toiling at the useless soil. The songs of the sailors rang in his ears, the tobacco smoke blinded his eyes, the brandy seemed to mix with the blood in his veins.

The women danced with the sailors. Someone had found a concertina, and a fiddle with three strings. Crazy tunes broke into the air. The women had never danced before. They were whirled from their feet, their petticoats flying out behind them. The sailors laughed and sang, beating the measure with their feet upon the floor. The fishermen lolled stupidly against the walls, drunken, happy, careless of time. A sailor came across to Jane and smiled, holding out his arms. She danced with him, flushed, excited, eager to please. Faster, faster went the music, and faster flew their feet around the room. She felt his arm tighten round her waist, and was aware of the warmth of his body against hers. She could feel his breath upon her cheek. She raised her head and met his eyes. They looked into hers, seeing her naked, and he moistened his lips with his tongue. They smiled, reading each other's thoughts. An exquisite shudder, like the touch of a cool hand, ran through her. Her legs felt weak beneath her. She lowered her eyes, conscious of desire, and turned to see if Guthrie had noticed, guilty for the first time.

And the East Wind blew against the church, shaking the roof, and the surf broke and thundered on the shore.

The next day dawned the same, hot and relentless.

The wind did not weaken in its power, nor the sea lessen in its fury. The brig still rolled at her moorings amongst the fishing boats. The fishermen leant with the sailors against the harbour wall, drinking and smoking, without thought, without energy, cursing the wind. The women idled at their cooking, neglected their mending. They stood at the doors

9

of the cottages, new scarves round their shoulders, scarlet handkerchieves upon their heads, impatient with the children, restless, waiting for a smile.

The day passed thus, and another night, and yet another day. The sun shone, the sea shuddered and crashed, the wind blew. No one left the harbour to fish, no one worked on the land. There seemed no shade on the island, the grass lay brown and withered, the leaves hung parched and despondent from the few trees. Night fell once more and the wind had not ceased. Guthrie sat in the cottage, his head between his hands, his brain empty. He felt ill and tired, like a very old man. Only one thing could prevent the sound of the wind from screaming in his ears and the heat of the sun from scorching his eyes. His lungs were dry, his throat ached. He staggered from the cottage and went down the hill to the church, where the sailors and the fishermen lay in heaps upon the floor, the brandy running from their mouths. He flung himself amongst them and drank greedily, senselessly, giving himself to it, forgetting the wind and the sea.

Jane closed the cottage door behind her and ran out onto the cliffs. The tall grass bathed her ankles and the wind leapt through her hair. It sang in her ears, a triumphant call. The sea flung itself upon the rocks below and loose flecks of foam scattered up towards her. She knew that if she waited he would come to her from the chapel. All day his eyes had followed her as she walked amongst the sailors by the harbour wall. Nothing mattered but this. Guthrie was drunk, asleep, forgotten, but here on the cliffs the stars shone upon her, and the East Wind blew. A dark shadow appeared from behind a clump of trees. For one moment she was afraid. One moment only.

'Who are you?' she called, but her voice fled to the wind.

The sailor came towards her. He flung off her clothes with deft, accustomed fingers; she put her hands before her eyes to hide her face. He laughed, and buried his lips in her hair. She stood then with arms outstretched, waiting, naked and unashamed, like a white phantom, broken and swept by the wind. Down in the chapel the men shouted and sang. They fought amongst themselves, mad with drink. One fisherman threw a knife and pinned his brother against the wall. He writhed like a serpent, screaming with pain.

Guthrie rose to his feet. 'Quiet, you dogs!' he shouted. 'Can you not drink in peace, and leave men to their dreams? Is it like this you wait for the wind to change?'

Jeers and laughter drowned his voice. A man pointed a trembling finger at him. 'Aye, talk of peace, Guthrie, you weak-limbed fool. With your wife even now shaming your bed with a stranger. We'll have new blood in the island, I reckon.' A chorus of voices joined in, laughing, and they pointed at him. 'Aye, Guthrie, look to your wife!'

He leapt at them with a cry of rage, smashing their faces. But they were too many for him, they threw him from the chapel, flinging him onto the rough quayside. He lay stunned for a moment, then shook himself like a dog and rose to his feet. So Jane was a wanton. Jane had deceived him. He remembered his wife's body, white and slim. A haze of madness came over him, mingled with hatred and desire. He stumbled through the darkness, up the hill to the cottage. There was no light in any of the windows; the rooms were empty.

'Jane,' he called, 'Jane, where be ye hidin' with your damned cur lover?' No one answered. Sobbing with rage, he tore

11

an axe from the wall – a great clumsy tool, used for chopping firewood. 'Jane,' he called once more, 'come out, will ye?'

His voice was powerless against the wind that shook the walls of the cottage. He crouched by the door and waited, the axe in his hands. Hours passed and he sat in a stupor, awaiting her return. Before dawn she came, pale and trembling, like a lost thing. He heard her footfall on the path. A twig snapped under her feet. The axe uplifted.

'Guthrie,' she screamed, 'Guthrie, let me alone, let me alone.' She spread her hands in supplication, but he pushed them aside and brought the axe down upon her head, crumpling her, smashing her skull. She fell to the ground, twisted, unrecognisable, ghastly. He leant over her, peering at her body, breathing heavily. The blood ran before his eyes. He sat down by her side, his senses swimming, his mind vacant. He fell into a drunken sleep, his head pillowed on her breast.

When he awoke, sober, himself again, he found her dead body at his feet. He gazed at it in horror, not understanding. The axe was still upon the floor. He lay stunned, sick and frightened, unable to move. Then he listened, as if for an accustomed sound. All was silent. Something had changed. The wind. He could no longer hear the wind.

He staggered to his feet and looked out upon the island. The air was cool. Rain had fallen while he slept. From the southwest blew a cool, steady breeze. The sea was grey and calm. Far on the horizon lay a black dot, her white sails outlined against the sky.

The brig had gone with the morning tide.

The Doll

Foreword.
The following pages were found in a shabby pocket book, very much sodden and discoloured by salt water, tucked away between the crevices of a rock in — Bay.

Their owner has never been traced, and the most diligent enquiries have failed to discover his identity. Either the wretched man drowned himself near the spot where he hid his pocket book, and his body has been lost at sea; or he is still wandering about the world trying to forget himself and his tragedy.

Some of the pages of his story were so damaged by exposure as to render them completely illegible; thus there are many gaps, and much of it seems without sequence, including the abrupt and unsatisfactory termination.

I have placed three dots between sentences when words or lines were undecipherable. Whether the wild improbabilities of the story are true, or whether the whole is but the hysterical product of a diseased mind, we shall never know. My sole reason for publishing these pages is to satisfy the entreaties of many friends who have been interested in my discovery.

Signed. Dr E. Strongman.

— Bay,
  S. England.

I want to know if men realise when they are insane. Sometimes I think that my brain cannot hold together, it is filled with too much horror – too great a despair.

And there is no one; I have never been so unutterably alone. Why should it help me to write this? . . . Vomit forth the poison in my brain.

For I am poisoned, I cannot sleep, I cannot close my eyes without seeing his damned face . . .

If only it had been a dream, something to laugh over, a festered imagination.

It's easy enough to laugh, who wouldn't crack their sides and split their tongues with laughing. Let's laugh till the blood runs from our eyes – there's fun, if you like. No, it's the emptiness that hurts, the breaking up of everything inside me.

If I could feel, I should have followed her to the ends of the earth, no matter how she pleaded or how she loathed me. I should have taught her what it is to be loved by a man – yes – a man, and I would have thrown his filthy battered body from the window, watched him disappear for ever, his evil scarlet mouth distorted . . .

It's the hot feeling that has filled me, the utter incapacity to reason.

And I am deceiving myself when I say she would have come to me. I did not follow her because I knew that it

14

was hopeless. She would never have loved me – she will never love any man.

Sometimes I can think of it all dispassionately, and I pity her. She misses so much – so much – and no one will ever know the truth. What was her life before I knew her, what is it now?

Rebecca – Rebecca, when I think of you with your pale earnest face, your great wide fanatical eyes like a saint, the narrow mouth that hid your teeth, sharp and white as ivory, and your halo of savage hair, electric, dark, uncontrolled – there has never been anyone more beautiful. Who will ever know your heart, who will ever know your mind?

Intense, restrained, and soul-less; for you must be soul-less to have done what you have done. You have that fatal quality of silence – of a tight repression that suggests a hidden fire – yes, a burning fire unquenchable. What have I not done with you in dreams, Rebecca?

You would be fatal to any man. A spark that lights, and does not burn itself, a flame fanning other flames.

What did I love in you but your indifference, and the suggestions that lay beneath your indifference?

I loved you too much, wanted you too much, had for you too great a tenderness. Now all of this is like a twisted root in my heart, a deadly poison in my brain. You have made of me a madman. You fill me with a kind of horror, a devastating hate that is akin to love – a hunger that is nausea. If only I could be calm and clear for one moment – one moment only . . .

I want to make a plan – an orderly arrangement of dates.

It was at Olga's studio first, I think. I can remember how it rained outside, and the rain made dirty streaks on the window-pane. The room was full, a lot of people were talking by the piano – Vorki was there, they were trying to make him sing, and Olga was screaming with laughter.

I always hated the hard thin reed of her laugh. You were sitting – Rebecca was sitting on a stool by the fire.

Her legs were twisted under her, and she looked like an elf, a sort of boy.

Her back was turned to me, and she wore a funny little fur cap on her head. I remember being amused at her position, I wanted to see her face. I called out to Olga to introduce me.

'Rebecca,' she said, 'Rebecca, show yourself.' . . . flinging off her cap as she turned. Her hair sprung from her head like a savage, her eyes opened wide – and she smiled at me, biting her lip.

I can remember sitting down on the floor beside her, and talking, talking – what does it matter what I said, dull stuff, nonsense of course, but she spoke breathlessly, with a sort of constrained eagerness. She did not say much, she smiled . . . eyes of a visionary, of a fanatic – they saw too much, demanded too much – one lost oneself in them, and became incapable of resistance. It was like drowning. From the moment I saw her then I was doomed. I left her, and came away, and walked down the embankment like a drunkard. Faces spluttered up at me, and shoulders brushed me, I was aware of dim lights reflected on wet pavements, and the hazy throb of traffic – through it all were her eyes and her wild impossible hair, her slim body like a boy . . . all coming clear now, I can see each event as it happened, each moment of the game. I went to Olga's again and she was there.

She came right up to me and said 'Do you care for

music?' gravely, like a child. Why did she say this, I don't know, there was no one at the piano – I answered vaguely, and noticed the colour of her skin, pale coffee, and clear, clear as water.

She was dressed in brown, some sort of velvet I think, with a red scarf round her neck.

Her throat was very long and thin, like a swan's. I remember thinking how easy it would be to tighten the scarf and strangle her. I imagined her face when dying – her lips parted, and the enquiring look in her eyes – they would show white, but she would not be afraid. All this in the space of a moment, and while she was talking to me. I could drag very little from her. She was a violinist apparently, an orphan, and lived alone in Bloomsbury.

Yes, she had travelled much, she said, and especially in Hungary. She had lived in Budapest for three years, studying music. She did not care for England, she wanted to go back to Budapest. It was the only city in the world.

'Rebecca,' someone called, and she glanced over her shoulder with a smile. How much could I write about Rebecca's smile! It was so vivid, so intensely alive, and yet apart, unearthly, it had no relation to anything one said. Her eyes would be transfigured as if by a shaft of silver.

She left early that day, and I crossed the room to ask Olga about her. I was in an agony of impatience to know everything. Olga could tell me little. 'She comes from Hungary,' she said, 'no one knows who were her parents, Jewish, I imagine. Vorki brought her here. He found her in Paris, playing the violin in one of those Russian cafés. She won't have anything to do with him though, she lives entirely alone. Vorki says her talent is marvellous, if she only goes on there will be no one to touch her. But she won't work, she doesn't seem to care. I heard her at Vorki's flat – it sent cold shivers down my spine. She stood at the end of the room, looking like something off another planet, – her hair sticking out, a sort of fur bush round her head, and she played. The notes were weird, haunting, I've never known anything quite like it, it's impossible to describe.'

Once again I left Olga's studio in a dream, with Rebecca's face dancing before my eyes. I too could see her playing the violin – she would stand straight and firm as a child, her eyes wide open, her lips parted in a smile.

She was to play at Vorki's flat the following evening, and I went to hear her. Olga had not exaggerated, with all her palpable, shallow insincerity. I sat like a drugged man, incapable of movement. I don't know what she played, but it was shattering – stupendous. I was not aware of anything but that I and Rebecca were together – out of the world, away, lost – lost in unutterable bliss. We were climbing, then flying, higher – higher.

At one time the violin seemed to protest, and it was as if she were refusing me, and I were pursuing her – then there came a torrent of sound, a medley of acceptance and denial, a confusion of notes in which were mingled desire and sweetness, and intolerable pleasure. I could feel my heart beating like the throb of some mighty vessel, and the blood pounded in my temples.

Rebecca was part of me, she was myself – it was too much, it was too glorious. We had reached the summit, we could go no farther, the sun seemed to strike into my eyes. I looked up – Rebecca was smiling at me, the violin broke on a note of exquisite beauty – it was fulfilment.

I leant back exhausted on the sofa, my senses swimming – it was too wonderful, too wonderful. Three minutes passed before I came fully conscious again. I felt as if I had plunged in the black abyss of eternity to sleep – and had come awake once more.

No one had noticed me, Vorki was handing round drinks, and Rebecca was sitting by the piano turning over some music. When they asked her to play again, she refused, she was tired, she said. They implored her so she took up her violin and played once more – something quite short, but very lovely and pure, like a child's prayer.

Later in the evening she came and sat beside me, for a few moments I was too moved to speak. Then I cursed myself for a fool, and turned to her, and looked into her face.

'You gave me a marvellous sensation when you played,' I told her, 'it was beautiful, intoxicating, I shall never forget it. You have a rare – no – a very dangerous talent.' She was silent, and then spoke in her restrained, breathless little voice. 'I played for you,' she said, 'I wanted to see what it was like to play to a man.' Her words bewildered me, they seemed utterly inexplicable. She was not lying, her eyes looked straight into mine, and she was smiling.

'What do you mean?' I asked her. 'Have you never played for anyone before, do you use your gift just to satisfy yourself? I don't understand.'

'Perhaps,' she said slowly, 'perhaps, it's like that, I can't explain.'

'I want to see you again,' I told her, 'I'd like to come and see you alone, where we can talk, really talk. I've thought about you ever since I saw you in Olga's studio, you knew that, didn't you? That's why you played to me tonight, wasn't it?'

I wanted to drag the answer from her lips, I wanted to force her to say yes. She shrugged her shoulders, she refused to be definite, it was exasperating.

'I don't know,' she said, 'I don't know.' Then I asked for her address, and she gave it to me. She was busy, she would not be able to see me until the end of the week. The party broke up soon after and she disappeared.

The days that passed seemed interminable, I could not wait to see her again. I thought about her ceaselessly.

On Friday I could stand it no longer, so I went to her. She lived in an odd sort of a house somewhere in Bloomsbury. She rented the top floor as a flat. The outlook was dull and dreary, I wondered how she could bear to live there.

She opened the door to me herself, and took me into a large bare room like a studio, with an oil-stove burning. I was struck by the cheerlessness of it, but she did not seem to notice anything, and made me sit down in a shabby arm-chair.

'This is where I practise,' Rebecca told me, 'and have my meals. It's a bright room, don't you think?' I said nothing to this and then she went to a cupboard and brought out some drinks, and a few stale biscuits. She took nothing herself.

I found her strange, detached – she seemed bored at my being there. Our conversation was forced and there were pauses. I found it impossible to say any of the things I wanted to say. She played to me for a while, but they were all classical things that I knew, and quite different from what she had played that evening at Vorki's.

Before I left she showed me round her tiny flat. There was a little scullery place she used for a kitchen, a poky bathroom, and her own small bedroom which was furnished like a nun's cell, quite plain and bare. There was another room leading from the studio, but she did not show me this. It was obviously a fair-sized room, as I saw the window from the street afterwards, and watched her draw the heavy curtains across it . . .

(*Note.* Here some pages were completely illegible, covered with blots, and discoloured. The narrative appears to continue in the middle of a sentence. Dr Strongman)

. . . 'not really cold,' she insisted, 'I've tried to explain to you that I'm odd in some ways, I've never met anyone to care for, I've never been in love. I've always disliked people rather than been attracted by them.' 'That doesn't explain your music.' I broke in impatiently. 'You play as if you knew everything – everything.'

I was becoming maddened by her indifference, it was not natural but calculated; she always gave me the impression of concealment. I felt I should never discover what was in her mind, whether she was like a child asleep, a flower before it has blossomed – or whether she was lying to me throughout, in which case every man would have been her lover – every man.

I was tortured by doubt and jealousy, the thought of other men was driving me insane. And she gave me no relief, she would look at me with her great pale eyes, pure as water, until I could swear that she was untouched – and yet, and yet? A look, a smile, and back would come my torture and my misery. She was impossible, she evaded everything, and yet it was this fatal quality of restraint that tore at me and broke at me, until my love for her became an obsession, a terrible driving force.

21

I asked Olga about her, asked Vorki, asked everyone who knew her. No one could tell me anything, anything.

I'm forgetting days and weeks as I write this, nothing seems to have any sequence for me, it's like rising from the dead, it's like being reincarnated from dust and ashes to live it again, to live my whole cursed life again — for what was my life before I loved Rebecca, where was I, who was I?

I had better write that Sunday now, Sunday that was really the end; and I didn't know it, I thought it was the beginning. I was like someone walking in the dark, no, walking in the light with his eyes open and not seeing — deliberately blinding himself.

Sunday, day of hollow and mistaken happiness. I went to her flat about nine in the evening. She was waiting for me. She was dressed in scarlet — like Mephistopheles, odd strange clothes, that only Rebecca could wear. She seemed excited, intoxicated — she ran about the room like an elf.

Then she sat down at my feet with her legs tucked under her, and held out her thin brown hands to the stove. She laughed and giggled childishly, she reminded me of a mischievous child planning some naughtiness.

Then all at once she turned to me, her face pale, her eyes strangely alight. She said, 'Is it possible to love someone so much, that it gives one a pleasure, an unaccountable pleasure to hurt them? To hurt them by jealousy I mean, and to hurt oneself at the same time. Pleasure and pain, an equal mingling of pleasure and pain, just as an experiment, a rare sensation?'

She puzzled me, but I tried to explain to her what was meant by Sadism. She seemed to understand, and nodded her head thoughtfully once or twice.

22

Then she rose and went slowly across the room to the door I had never yet seen opened. She looked oddly pale as she stood there, her mass of queer savage hair springing from her head, her hand on the knob of the door. 'I want to introduce you to Julio,' she said. I left my chair and went towards her, I had no idea of what she was talking about. She took my hand and then opened the door. I saw a low round-shaped room, whose walls were draped with some sort of velvet hangings as if to deaden any sound, and long thick curtains were drawn across the window. There was a log fire, but it had burnt very low. Near the fireplace was a divan, covered with cushions thrown anyhow, and the only light came from a small shaded lamp, thus leaving the room in a half darkness.

There was one chair in the room, and this was facing the divan.

Something was sitting in the chair. I felt an eerie cold feeling in my heart, as if the room were haunted. 'What is it?' I whispered.

Rebecca took the lamp and held it over the chair. 'This is Julio,' she said softly. I stepped closer, and saw what I took to be a boy of about sixteen, dressed in a dinner jacket, shirt and waistcoat, and long Spanish trousers.

His face was the most evil thing I have ever seen. It was ashen pale in colour, and the mouth was a crimson gash, sensual and depraved. The nose was thin, with curved nostrils, and the eyes were cruel, gleaming and narrow, and curiously still. They seemed to stare right through one – the eyes of a hawk. The hair was sleek and dark, brushed right back from the white forehead.

It was the face of a satyr, a grinning hateful satyr.

Then I was aware of a strange feeling of disappointment,

23

a helpless sensation of not understanding, of dumb incredulity.

There was no boy sitting in the chair. It was a doll. Human enough, damnably lifelike, with a foul distinctive personality, but a doll.

Only a doll. The eyes stared into mine without recognition, the mouth leered foolishly.

I looked at Rebecca, she was watching my face.

'I don't see,' I said, 'what's the point of all this? Where did you get this loathsome toy? Are you having a joke with me?' I spoke sharply, I felt uneasy and cold. The next moment the room was in darkness, she had turned out the lamp. I felt her arms round my neck, and her mouth upon mine.

'Now shall I tell you I love you?' she whispered, 'shall I?'

A hot wave of something swept over me, the floor seemed to swing beneath my feet. She clung to me and kissed my throat, I could feel her fingers at the back of my neck. I let her hands wander over my body, and she kissed me again. It was devastating – it was madness – it was like death.

I don't know how long we stood there, I don't remember anything, words, or thoughts, or dreams – only the silence of that dark room, the feeble glow of the fire, the beating of my heart – the singing in my ears – and Rebecca – Rebecca—. When, – and whether hours had passed or years I cannot tell – when I raised my eyes above her head I looked straight into his eyes – his damned doll's eyes.

They seemed to squint at me and leer, one eyebrow was cocked, and his crimson treacherous mouth was twisted at the corner. I wanted to leap at it, and smash its beastly grinning face, trample on its sordid human body. Was Rebecca mad to keep such a toy, what was her motive, where had she found it? But she would not answer my questions.

'Come away,' she said, and dragged me from the room, back once more into the hard glaring light of the bare studio. 'You must go now,' she said breathlessly, 'it's late – I had forgotten.' I tried to take hold of her, once more, I wanted to kiss her again and again, she surely did not mean me to go now.

'Tomorrow,' she said impatiently, 'I promise you tomorrow, but not at the moment. I'm tired and bewildered – don't you see? Let me alone just for tonight, it's been too strong, I can't realise anything.'

She stamped her foot with impatience, she looked ill. I saw it was hopeless. I took my things and went – and walked, and walked – all night I think.

I watched the dawn break on Hampstead Heath, grey and sunless; heavy rain fell from a leaden sky.

My body was cold, but my brain was on fire. Once more I was certain that Rebecca had lied to me – from the moment she kissed me I knew that she had lied to me.

She had known five, ten, what matter the number, twenty lovers – and I was not one of them.

No, I was not one of them.

I found myself near Camden Town, buses rumbled along the streets; it was still raining, people straggled past me, their figures bent under umbrellas.

I found a taxi somewhere, and went home. I got into bed without undressing, and slept. I slept for hours. When I awoke it was dark once more; it must have been about

25

six in the evening. I remember washing mechanically, and then once more walking in the direction of Bloomsbury.

I reached the flat and rang at her bell.

She let me in without a word, and then sat down in the studio before the oil stove. I told her I was going to be her lover. She said nothing. There were red rims under her eyes as if she had been crying, and thin lines round her mouth. I bent towards her to kiss her, but she pushed me away.

She began to speak rapidly.

'You must forget what happened last night. Today I realise I made a mistake. I'm not well, I haven't slept. All this has worried me considerably. You must leave me alone.'

I tried to seize her, and break down her iron restraint. It was like hammering at an iron wall. She lay cold and still in my arms. Her mouth was icy. I left her in despair. Then followed a week of doubt and torture. Sometimes she sat apart from me without a word, sometimes I could have sworn that she loved me. And she would not let me touch her, she was not in the mood she said. I must wait until she wanted me again. I must wait in suspense, in agony. She never mentioned Julio. We never went into that room again. I asked her what she had done with him. I wanted to know what was at the back of it all. She would answer evasively and change the subject. It was useless to press her. She was maddening. She was intolerable.

And yet I could not keep away from her. I could not live without her.

One evening she would be gentle and affectionate. She would sit at my feet and talk about her music, about her future plans. She was always changing. She was never the same.

I felt hopeless. My position was ridiculous — but what was I to do? She had become a madness to me — an obsession.

I've now come to the last evening, the very last. Then crash — blankness — the depths of hell — and desolation — utter desolation.

Let me get it clear — when was it, what time was it? Seven, eight perhaps. I can't remember. I was leaving the flat and she came to the door with me.

She suddenly put her arms round me and kissed me. . . . There have been men in arid deserts where the sun has so disfigured them that they have become things of horror — parched and blackened, twisted and torn. Their eyes run blood, their tongues are bitten through — and then they come upon water.

I know, because I was one of their number.

Laugh at all these comparisons, call me a madman, but the laugh is on my side.

There are women — but you have not kissed Rebecca, you cannot know.

You are a fool asleep. You have never begun to imagine . . .

(*Note.* Much of this seems completely unintelligible, and the quarter page that follows consists of nothing but broken sentences and half formed ideas. Then the narrative continues.)

It was shattering. She let me kiss her again and again. I took her face in my hands and looked down into her eyes.

'Who were your lovers?' I said. 'How often did you kiss them like that? Who taught you to kiss them like that? Who was the first, the very first? Tell me.'

27

A haze of fury was before my eyes, my hands shook.

'I swear to you that you are the first man I have ever kissed. I swear to you there has been no man before you. Never. Never.'

She looked straight at me. Her voice was firm. I saw that she was speaking the truth.

'Now you must go,' she said, 'tomorrow you shall come, and then we shall have so much to tell each other, so much.'

She smiled at me. I saw right through her wall of restraint, right through ice to the flame, the hidden fire.

I remember leaving the flat, and having dinner somewhere. My head was on fire. I seemed to walk among the gods. It was incredible that Rebecca should love me, it was incredible that I should know such happiness. I wanted to shout. I wanted to chuck myself off a roof.

I went home, and paced up and down the room. I couldn't sleep, every nerve in my body seemed alive.

Then suddenly, at midnight, I could stand it no longer. I had to go to Rebecca, I had to.

I felt my love for her was so strong that she would know. She would wait for me. She would understand. She would have to understand.

I don't know how I got to her flat. Seconds seemed to flash by, and I was standing outside in the street, gazing up at the windows.

I persuaded the night porter to let me in, he was half asleep and he let me pass upstairs. I listened outside her door – not a sound came from within. It might have been the entrance to a tomb.

I put my hand on the door knob, and turned it slowly. To my surprise it was not locked – Rebecca must have forgotten to turn the key after I left.

I stepped inside, everything was in darkness. 'Rebecca,' I called softly, 'Rebecca.' No answer.

The door of her bedroom was open, there was no one inside.

Then I went into the kitchen and the bathroom, both were empty.

Then I knew. Something gripped my heart, cold, clammy fear.

I looked towards that other room – his room – Julio's room.

I knew that Rebecca was in there, with the doll – with Julio.

I felt my way across the room and beat against the door. It was locked. I kicked against the panel, and tore at it with my nails. It gave way beneath my weight. I heard a cry of fury from Rebecca, and she turned on the lamp.

Oh! Christ, I shall never forget her eyes, the terrible light – the unholy rapture in her eyes, and her ashen – ashen face.

I saw everything – the room, the divan – I knew everything. I was seized with deadly sickness – a terrible despair.

And all the time his vile filthy face was looking at me. His eyes never left me, staring with a lifeless, glassy immobility. The wet crimson mouth was sneering – the sleek dark hair hung in streaks across his cheek. He was a machine – something worked by screws – he was not alive, not human – but terrible, ghastly.

And Rebecca turned to me. Her voice was cold – apart – unearthly.

'And you expect me to love you. Don't you see that I can't – I can't? How can I care for you, or any man? Go away, leave me. I loathe you. I loathe you all. I don't need you. I don't want you.'

Something cracked inside my heart. I turned away. I left them. I left them alone. I ran into the street – tears were pouring down my face – I sobbed aloud – I shook my fist at the stars . . .

And that is all, there is no more to say, no more to tell. I went the next day and she had gone, they had both gone. No one knew where she was. I asked everyone I saw – no one could tell me.

Everything is dim, everything is useless. I shall never see Rebecca again – no one will see her again. It will always be Rebecca and Julio. Days will come, and nights, and nothing – they will haunt me – I shall never sleep – I'm cursed. I don't know what I'm saying, what I'm writing. What am I going to do? Oh! God, what am I going to do? I can't live – I can't cope . . .

And Now to God the Father

The Reverend James Hollaway, Vicar of St Swithin's, Upper Chesham Street, was looking at his profile in the glass. The sight was pleasing to him, so much so that he lingered a considerable time before he laid the mirror back upon the dressing-table.

He saw a man of about fifty-five years of age, who looked younger, with a high forehead and magnificent iron-grey hair, that was apt to curl slightly at the temples.

The nose was straight, the mouth narrow and sensitive, and he had been told that his deep-set eyes could be in turn humorous, dangerous, and inspired. He was tall and broad-shouldered; he carried his head a little to one side, and his powerful chin was tilted in the air.

To some this was his fascination, this inquiring, conceited angle of the head; to others it was the rich tones of his ever-changing voice, the strong capable hands, the slow lilting walk that was the secret of his tremendous attraction.

Yet all these were as nothing compared to his charm of manner, his wit, his talent for making the shyest person feel at ease.

Women adored him; he was so broad-minded, so tolerant, and he always gave the impression that he understood them far better than they did themselves. Besides, he was always so delightfully intimate. Men found him a surprisingly good companion; his wine was excellent; he never talked about religion, and he ever had a fund of damned amusing stories. It was all these qualities combined that made him the most popular preacher in London.

He was bound in time to become a bishop. St Swithin's was frequented by the very best people. The fashionable thing to do was to attend Mass on Sunday mornings, and if possible to get an invitation back to lunch at the Vicar's exquisitely furnished Georgian house that adjoined the church.

Here one was sure to find a crowd of well-known people: a leading politician, a couple of famous actresses, a rising young painter, and of course a sprinkling of titles.

Everyone agreed that 'Jim' Hollaway was a perfect host, and his conversation was as clever as his sermons. He was careful never to speak about God, or anything embarrassing, but was ever willing to discuss last night's new play, the latest book, the newest fashion, and even the most recent scandal. He made a show of his excessive modernity, and besides being a keen poker-player, and an enthusiastic dancer, he delighted the younger generation by the freedom of his expressions. There was something so very original in the idea of being shocked by a clergyman. In church of course he was different, and this they appreciated.

With his tall figure, his striking voice and eyes, his eloquent gestures, the whole effect was rather wonderful. People soon forgave him his High Church tendencies, and the celebration of Mass instead of the usual eleven-o' clock Matins. Also there was more to watch.

Men went to listen to the singing and because it was the thing to do; women went for the flowers and the lighted candles, for the agreeable emotional sensation that was produced by the smell of incense, and above all because they were half in love with the Vicar.

When they had summoned up enough courage to go to confession they were overwhelmed by his gentleness, his discretion, and above all by his apparent understanding. Some of the more intense of his congregation went to his Thursday-afternoon teas.

Here at last religion was discussed, but the Vicar made his gatherings so free from awkwardness that there was never the slightest feeling of restraint. He was a great comforter of uneasy souls, and portrayed God in a very gentle light, insisting upon His immense humanity.

They learnt with relief that God not only pardoned but was fond of sinners, in fact it seemed that He preferred them to the ninety-and-nine just men. Of course the Vicar implied that they were all as yet but seeds in the mighty growth of evolution, and that some time, very far hence, they would know perfection and look upon beauty in its greatest form, but in the meanwhile – well, in the meanwhile one lived and one naturally sinned, and received absolution and sinned again, and one lived according to one's merits and station-in-the-world.

One must also bear in mind that conditions were very different from what they were nearly two thousand years ago. All of which was a very consoling philosophy. It was rendered so sacred, too, when spoken in the Vicar's soft melodious voice; and when he turned his beautiful sympathetic eyes upon each member of the party in turn they thought he was addressing them especially, and could read the secrets of their hearts.

Later, when he met them casually at the Duchess of

Attleborough's Thé Dansant, or in the front row of the stalls at a first night, he would smile his wonderful sense-disturbing smile, and whisper some amusing description in their ears, but they felt that his eyes were saying 'I know, I understand.'

He was unmarried, of course, and yet there was always the hopeless terrible longing that perhaps one day – however, he had fallen for no one yet, though rumour, forgetting the sanctity of the cloth, had linked his name with those of many beautiful and always noble ladies.

As the Vicar replaced the glass upon the dressing-table, and ran his hand carelessly, boyishly he considered, through his sleek grey hair, he smiled a little to himself. Yes, he had worn well, he was still a very good-looking man.

He went downstairs, and into his study. The room was large and furnished in remarkable taste. On his desk was a large portrait of one of England's most beautiful actresses; on it was written 'Jim, with my love, Mona,' and the date of a summer two years ago.

The mantelpiece was adorned with Her Grace of Attleborough, 'Your very affectionate Norah,' and on a little table by the window was a striking study of Lady Eustace Carey-Slater, and her dashing signature 'Attaboy! from Jane.' The Vicar ran through his letters, and then rang the bell for his butler.

'Any message for me, Wells?' he asked.

'Yes, sir; two ladies called who said they were in terrible circumstances, and would very much like to have a few words with you. I told them you were very busy and would they see the Curate.'

The Vicar nodded his approval – some of these women were a pest.

34

'Then Lord Cranleigh rang up, and asked to see you some time this morning. I told him to come over at once, as you were not engaged.'

'Quite right, Wells. That's all, thank you. Bring in the paper, will you?' The man was an admirable servant.

While he was waiting for his visitor he let his eye run over the list of births, marriages, and deaths. By Jove, Kitty Durand was going to be married, and she had never told him. He must send her a present, he supposed, and a letter of congratulation. 'Kitty, you wicked child, what's the meaning of this? You deserve to be spanked. Only eighteen! Your fiancé is a lucky fellow, and I'm going to tell him so. Bless you both.'

Something like that would do, and a cocktail set from Goodes.

'Yes, Wells, what is it?'

'Lord Cranleigh,' said the butler, and closed the door behind a boy of about twenty-two, with fair hair and a pleasantly weak face.

'I say, sir, this is most awfully decent of you; can you really spare me a few moments?'

'Come and sit down, young fellow, and take your time,' said the Vicar, at once assuming his manner of easy comradeship, and pushing forward a box of cigarettes. He sat down in front of his desk, crossed his legs, and prepared to listen, while the boy flung himself into an easy-chair.

'The fact is, sir, I'm in the devil of a mess,' he began awkwardly. 'I hadn't the slightest idea who to turn to, and then I remembered you. Of course in the ordinary way I should never dare to ask the advice of a parson, but you're different. You're so, excuse my cheek, you're so, well, damn broad-minded!'

The Vicar's heart warmed to the usual praise. 'I've been young myself once,' he nodded sympathetically, and he let his eyes wander vaguely towards the various photographs in the room. This boy must be made to understand that he was talking to no raw hand, in fact—

'It's about a girl,' Cranleigh went on. 'A girl I met at Oxford last term, just before the long vac. She was nobody, you know, just acted as companion to some old lady, and I met her first of all when I was fooling about on the river. She was with a friend, and I was with another fellow, so we all sort of chummed up. Well, after that I began to see her pretty often, and got desperately keen on her. Of course I dare say I wouldn't have looked at her if I'd been in London, but up there it's different. She was mad about me too, though I say it myself, and then – oh, Lord, I'm afraid I made a colossal ass of myself. Well, sir, I lost my head one night. I don't know how it happened, but it did – we were in a boat, and it was a glorious evening, and—'

'I know,' said the Vicar, his voice full of meaning; 'I was at Oxford too, over twenty years ago.'

The boy smiled, it was being easier than he expected. 'Well, you understand me, sir, I kind of couldn't help myself. Then very soon afterwards we came down, and I didn't see her again. Last week I got a letter from her; it was pretty awful, and she said she was going to have a baby.'

The Vicar sighed gently. 'Yes?' he asked.

'Of course I arranged to meet her, last Tuesday evening, and it's absolutely true, sir; she'd been to a doctor and everything. I was in a terrible state, and said I'd give her money and help her to get away somewhere; but – this is the awful part – she doesn't want money, she wants me to marry her.'

The Vicar raised his eyebrows. 'And what did you say to her?' he inquired.

'Well, naturally, I said it was impossible. How could I marry her? She's pretty and sweet, but I'm not sure she's even a lady, and I don't really love her. Besides, what on earth would the family say? When the old man dies I come into the title, and I've got to think of all that, although it sounds beastly snobbish. It would be madness to marry Mary, you must see my point?'

'My dear fellow, of course I do. There shall be no question of marriage as far as I'm concerned. And you say she refuses money?' His tone was brisk now, alert, that of a shrewd man of the world.

'Absolutely, sir; she went white when I suggested it. Apparently she doesn't seem to mind having the baby, she says she'll live for it, and she wants me to marry her so as to give it a name. She's still most awfully in love with me, and she doesn't seem to understand that I don't care any longer. If she goes to my people there will be the most colossal row. Thank heaven, she hasn't told a soul yet. Look here, sir, what on earth am I going to do?'

The Vicar was thinking rapidly. If he helped him out of this mess the boy would naturally be very grateful. He knew the family were rich, and the Earl was said to be in a wretched state of health. Cranleigh Castle was one of the beauty spots of England, he would be invited often: the Countess herself was an ardent politician – yes, everything would be comparatively easy. He rose from his chair, and going over to the boy he laid his hand on his shoulder. 'My dear chap,' he said, 'if you will trust me I am certain

I can manage the whole wretched business for you. There is no need for your family to know, we have your future position to think of; as for the girl, she will understand the whole situation when I have explained it tactfully to her. I will look after her. Don't worry any more about it; all I want you to do is to give me her address.'

'Mary Williams, sir. She's staying in a boarding-house in St John's Wood, it's on the telephone under the name of Datchett – that's her sister, she keeps the place. Oh! good Lord, you are the greatest brick; I don't know how I'm ever going to thank you enough.'

The Vicar smiled and held out his hand. 'It's only because I understand so well what you have gone through,' he said gently.

The man must have been a bit of a dog in his day, thought the boy; odd for a clergyman. 'I think I'll try and get away for a bit, until it's all blown over; but don't forget you've got to come down to Cranleigh directly I come back – we'll have a shot at the birds.'

When he had gone the Vicar went back into his study, and lifted the telephone receiver. He believed in doing things on the spot.

He looked up the number in the book.

'Is that Mrs Datchett's? Could I possibly speak to Miss Williams? Yes. Thank you . . . Hullo? Is that Miss Williams speaking? My name is Hollaway, James Hollaway. I'm the Vicar of St Swithin's, Chesham Street. I'm a great friend of Lord Cranleigh's. He has just left me . . . Yes. Would you be so good as to come and see me this evening at six o'clock? I should very much like a little talk with you, I wish to help you. Yes, he has told me everything. No, you have nothing to be frightened of. Then that is settled? Twenty-two Upper Chesham Street. Thank you. Good-bye.'

He hung up the receiver, and wandering to his desk he glanced at *The Times*.

Hallo, George Winnersly was dead at last. He must write to Lola. She was getting a bit *passée* now, of course, but she was still lovely. Funny the way she went religious all of a sudden. Must have come as a sort of anti-climax. She was always at St Swithin's at one time; he could remember once – However, that was all over.

He began to run over in his mind conventional phrases of consolation: 'immeasurably grieved,' 'unspeakable loss,' and 'the consolation of God.'

He yawned a little as he took up his pen.

'My dear daughter-in-Christ,' he began.

'Hollaway, you're a regular mascot, and I don't mind telling you I feel a lot more sure of myself now I've had this talk with you. Have a cigar?'

The Vicar declined. 'Sorry, but I haven't the time. I'm a busy man, you know, and I'm shortly due at a hospital in the slums. I'm very glad to have been of use to you, my dear Colonel, I understand so well what you are going through.'

His voice was full of the deepest sympathy.

The lunch at the Carlton had been a great success. His host was Colonel Edward Tracey, the Conservative candidate in the West Storeford by-election, and as polling day was on the following Monday the Colonel was nervous and agitated.

West Storeford was an important seat and the Colonel

a powerful man; if he was returned he would owe many of his votes to Hollaway, who had been one of his most ardent canvassers.

And he would be returned, of this the Vicar was certain. He was feeling very pleased with himself. 'There's not the slightest doubt about it,' he said warmly, 'the majority of voters in West Storeford are intelligent men and women. They know when they see a leader, and that's what they're after. Never mind if he's a Conservative, a Liberal, or a Socialist. Luckily for them you're a Conservative. My dear Colonel, I've heard you speak, and I know what I'm talking about. When you're in the House you're going to make those lazy fellows sit up. Lively times, eh! Wait till you are a Cabinet Minister!' He lowered his tone, and winked significantly.

The Colonel flushed all over his face with pleasure.

This parson was an amazingly good fellow, and when he was in Parliament he would remember to show his gratitude. He called for his bill, and the waiter brought the white slip of paper on a plate. The Vicar turned his head away discreetly, and bowed gallantly to a revue artiste who was just leaving the room. 'Pretty as ever, aren't you?' his eyes seemed to say. Then he rose from the table. 'My dear Colonel, I must leave you; I had no idea it was so late. This has been very delightful, and I shall be the first to congratulate you Monday night. No, don't bother to come out.'

He walked slowly across the room, his head a little to one side, his chin in the air.

Many people turned to watch him as he walked past.

The Vicar was aware of the disturbance he had caused. At the opening of the Royal Academy he had been taken for a distinguished actor.

He handed half-a-crown to the cloakroom attendant, and then stepped out into the street, where his Wolseley car was waiting. 'Drive to the East London Home for Disabled and Paralysed Men, and be quick about it,' he said to the chauffeur.

He leaned back, and let himself relax, as the car sped through the City. These weekly talks were rather a strain on the mind. The men were often surly and disinclined to listen, but he flattered himself he generally made an impression. He remembered last year at Pentonville, when a boy had taken a fancy to him. The whole thing had really been rather amusing, not only did he— but his car drew up in front of the Home, and his train of thought was interrupted.

He was greeted by a smiling nurse. 'We were afraid you were not coming, Mr Hollaway.'

'I had great difficulty in getting away at all, Sister. I was obliged to break up a very important political lunch, much to everyone's annoyance.'

There was no need to mention he had been the only guest, these nurses took everything so much for granted.

'We've got twenty-five of them up in the big ward, Mr Hollaway, and I must say I'm very glad you can spare them an hour. They get so dull and lifeless, I know you will cheer them up.'

The Vicar felt a little doubtful as he entered the ward. A quarter of the men were in bed, lying prone upon their backs, while the rest were in invalid-chairs, propped up with cushions.

A little doctor came forward hurriedly.

'My dear Vicar, this is too good of you. The men have been looking forward to your visit with the greatest pleasure. You've no idea,' he added in a lower tone, 'of the amount of good these talks can do. It puts new life into them, and it helps us more than I can say. They are very difficult sometimes, aren't they, Sister?'

He turned to the nurse, who nodded her agreement. The Vicar took her hand. 'I know so well what you must go through,' he murmured.

Then they left him alone with the men, and he plunged into his rôle of humorist and consoler. His cheerful voice and his delightful personality soon won the attention of the little group of men, doomed for the rest of their lives to lie on their backs, and to gaze at the ceiling.

'Because I'm a parson, there's no need for you to be shy of me, my lads,' he said, with his well-known infectious laugh. 'I've gone through a lot in my time, and I've talked and lived with every kind of fellow under the sun. Why, bless you, I feel exactly the same as all you men here, and I know and understand everything you don't tell your nurse and doctor.

'You don't know what a joy it is to me to come and talk to you this afternoon. It reminds me of the old days in France.' (Oh, shades of Paris!) Soon he had them all laughing at his stories, gleaned from every corner of the globe.

Good healthy humour, he told himself, and he warmed to his subject. Even the old chestnuts of four or five years ago were new here, he discovered. From these he went on to contemporary events. He discussed racing, boxing, cricket, and even politics with the more serious.

From politics it was an easy step to the apparent powerlessness of the Church to-day in State affairs, and from thence to religion, which he had really come to talk about.

42

The men of course had expected this; he was a parson, and now that they had heard his opinions on other subjects they were willing to listen to him in silence for the last half-hour that remained.

This afternoon the Vicar surpassed himself in eloquence, never had the life of the virtuous sounded more full of possibilities, never had the life of the sinner shone so dull in comparison.

'The world is so full of glorious opportunities to-day,' he said, in rich persuasive tones; 'we have every chance to better ourselves, to improve our minds, to give the best in exchange for the best.

'In enjoying the great facilities that are now open to us, I think we are apt to forget the Creator of it all.' The men blushed awkwardly, they were not quite sure what he was talking about. The Vicar felt he was swimming slightly out of their depth, so he returned to safer channels.

'What we forget,' he said, smiling his brilliant smile, 'is that Our Lord came to earth a man like ourselves. He felt all the pains and miseries that we feel. He underwent the troubles and vexations that we undergo. It is because we no longer remember this that we do not take our burdens to be lifted from us by One Who above all others can understand and help us. There has never been anyone so human as Christ. For well over thirty years He was a man amongst other men, a poor working man, the son of a carpenter. What do we know of that early life? Practically nothing. But we are sure it was a mixture of joy and sorrow such as falls to the lot of each of us. And in that part of His life that has been revealed to us through the medium of the Blessed Gospels (he lowered his voice suitably) there is full, unbounded proof that His feelings were those of a man.

'His adoration for Our Lady, the affection for Lazarus, the friendship for His disciples, the understanding of poor Magdalene – are these not all signs of His glorious Humanity? He was fond of animals and children; He talked with sinners.

'Remember the anger in the Temple and the distrust of the Pharisees; these all show those human qualities so dear to us. And lastly, in the Agony and Death on the Cross, were not His last cries those of a man?' The Vicar paused, a little out of breath. The men were obviously impressed, he had been victorious again.

Then a voice spoke from the far corner of the room. It came from a grumpy old man who had taken no part in the conversation.

'I thought Christ was the Son of God,' he said. There was an awkward silence, and for the moment the Vicar was a little taken aback.

Then 'He was,' he said gently; 'He was.' But it was too late: the spell had been broken. He left the room sensing defeat.

'Will you see a Miss Williams, sir?' said the butler, coming into the study shortly after six.

'Oh! yes, Wells, show her in. I was expecting her, but I forgot to tell you.'

The Vicar finished a much-needed whisky-and-soda, and placed the empty glass in a small cupboard built especially for that purpose.

Mary Williams came into the room.

She was small and dark, and though she was not looking

her best he could see that she was very pretty. She was neatly and simply dressed, and there were dark shadows under her eyes.

'Will you sit down?' he said courteously.

The girl obeyed silently, and waited for him to speak. He cleared his throat, the situation intrigued him.

'My dear child,' he began gently, 'I want you to look upon me as an elder brother, as one who knows the world far better than you do, and who every day tries to do his best, alas a very poor best, to lighten the responsibilities of those around him. And besides thinking of me as a brother, you must remember that I am a priest, and in that capacity I am capable of guarding over your spiritual as well as your earthly welfare.'

He paused. The girl made no reply, but stared at him with scared eyes.

'And thus,' he continued, 'I want you to tell me in your own way the story that Lord Cranleigh told me this morning; and spare no detail, however irksome it may be to you,' he added.

The girl blushed and lowered her eyes. 'I met Tommy first one day last term,' she began in a low tone. 'I was with a friend, we had hired a boat. He must have told you all this already. I was a companion to a Mrs Grey at the time, who lived in Oxford, and she went abroad alone as soon as the University went down for vacation.

'Tommy and the other man spoke to us that day because we were all sheltering under a tree during a heavy shower, and we soon got friendly, and laughed and joked together. We all had tea I remember.

'Then we arranged to meet again, and afterwards I always went out with Tommy whenever I could get away.

Very soon he told me that he loved me. I should not have listened to him, I suppose, but I could not help it; and when he kissed me for the first time I knew I loved him better than anything in the world. We used to make plans about all the wonderful things we would do in the vacation, and I thought – I didn't understand – I thought he meant he wanted to marry me.

'Every day I think I loved him a little more, and then – the night on the river – I forgot everything when he began to kiss me.

'He told you, I expect – I was so ashamed – I don't know how it happened,' she faltered.

The Vicar passed his hand over his mouth to hide his smile. Tame excuse – didn't know how it happened! Apparently not, or she would not be sitting there in front of him now.

'Yes,' he murmured, closing his eyes and sighing. 'Yes?'

'A day or two after that Tommy went down. Mrs Grey went abroad, and I stayed with friends in the country. I wrote to him nearly every day, but I never had a reply. I couldn't understand why he didn't write, I was so certain that he meant to marry me. I began to feel wretched and unhappy at the same time, my friends told me I was looking pale.

'Still no news from Tommy, though I knew he was in London, I saw something about his having been to a dance somewhere. Then one day I fainted – luckily no one was about – but I was frightened at once, and I went up to London in secret and saw a doctor.

'He – he told me what was the matter. I know it was wicked of me, but somehow I didn't seem to mind. I knew that Tommy would marry me now. I wrote to him, and went to stay with my sister in St John's Wood. When I saw Tommy he told me that he couldn't possibly marry me.

'I don't understand even now, my mind refuses to take it in. Please, Mr Hollaway, will you tell me what he said to you this morning? You see, I love him so terribly, and I can't do without him – now.'

The Vicar saw that she was ready to burst into a flood of helpless tears.

'Now, my dear, don't worry, but try and console yourself. I want you to sit quite quietly while I explain everything to you. I am going to help you, and I understand more than anyone just exactly what you have been through. But, at the same time, you must realise that God put us into the world so that we should know both joy and sorrow. If our joy has been sinful, then we must pay for it with tears and suffering.

'As we sow, so shall we reap.

'You are paying now for that night in the boat, and even for what occurred before.

'Has it ever struck you that you were guilty in the first place by being so friendly with a young man of whom you knew nothing?'

'I never thought,' stammered the girl.

'Of course not, and you must pay for that forgetfulness. You may not be aware of it, but if the world knew it would say that you had run after Lord Cranleigh, that you had visions of wealth, titles, and many other things besides.'

'It isn't true, it isn't true!' she gasped.

'Perhaps not, but if you told your story to anyone but me – to the boy's family, for instance – that's what they would say. They might even suspect that you are a girl of loose morals, and that to save yourself from prostitution you accuse a generous, impulsive young man of being the father of a child that is not really his.'

'No, no! How can you say that?'

'I am only saying what the world would say, who, I am afraid, is a very harsh critic.

'I want you to understand the position in which you will place yourself if you ask for justice at the hands of your lover's family. And then you must remember that Lord Cranleigh will very shortly become the Earl of Haversham. He will be a leading figure in society, he will have many duties and responsibilities, one of which will be to marry into some family as illustrious as his own. You say that you love him. Do you wish to wreck his career? Can you not see that the greatest proof of your love will be to go straight out of his life at once, before you can damage it any further?'

The girl was deathly pale now, the Vicar was afraid that she might faint.

'Yes,' she said slowly, 'I understand that I must give him up. What am I going to do?' She seemed quite stunned, and unable to think.

'I will see that you are amply provided for,' replied the Vicar, in deep generous tones. 'I know of two ladies who live in Wimbledon, they are gentle humane creatures, and they will look after you until the trouble is over.

'Your sister need know nothing about it, you can easily tell her you are with friends.

'When you are well again it would be better perhaps if you went abroad. I know of a missionary's wife in India, a charming, sympathetic woman, who will take you as a companion.'

'What about my baby?' asked the girl, with a queer frightened gleam in her eyes.

'That, of course, you must be prepared to give up also. The child shall be brought up in a beautiful Home in Surrey, of which I am one of the governors. Surely you must see the need of this?'

The girl rose from her chair.

'Thank you for all your trouble,' she said quietly. 'I think I had better go now. I will write if I want anything.'

The Vicar shrugged his shoulders. She did not seem particularly grateful to him, what more did she expect, he wondered.

'Good-bye, my child. I shall expect to hear from you in a few days, then.'

The door closed behind her. It had been a difficult interview, but it did not look as if she would bother Cranleigh any more.

The boy was well out of it anyway. He had rung up in the afternoon and left a message that he was going up to Scotland by the night train, and would probably stop there for about six weeks. He would soon forget the whole affair in Scotland. The Vicar glanced at the clock. Jove! he had no idea it was so late. He was due at the Duchess of Attleborough's little dinner-dance at eight-fifteen.

'James, you ought to be ashamed of yourself; how dare you make me laugh at your stories! Go away at once!'

The Duchess pushed the Vicar away from her with what she believed was a roguish gesture.

She was devoted to him, but she adored to pretend that he shocked her. He caught her hand, and would not let her escape.

'Norah,' he said reproachfully, 'how can you be so unkind to me? You place me next you on purpose, and then you complain when I try to amuse you. Perhaps you would rather I went away and sat beside that very charming young lady in pink who is looking at us?'

The girl, whom he had met at dinner for the first time, heard his remark and blushed. She thought the Vicar was terribly attractive.

The Duchess laughed indulgently. 'I won't allow you to say a word to her unless you behave yourself.'

He whispered something in her ear, and she went into peals of laughter. 'No, no; you are quite hopeless, and then you expect me to take you seriously when I come to St Swithin's. What are you going to preach about to-morrow?'

'Haven't decided yet,' he answered carelessly.

It was always a good pose of his that he never prepared his sermons. The Duchess shook her head at him, and very soon after she gave the signal to rise.

'The band has come,' she announced, 'and you men have got to come up and dance. I give you ten minutes down here and no more.'

The men laughed, and rose clumsily from their chairs. As soon as she had left the room, followed by a little crowd of lovely women, they sat down again, leant back comfortably, and began to discuss their hostess. The women whose husbands were not present were picked to pieces, physically and morally, while those who were received just the right amount of flattery and attention.

Someone made a few witty remarks about a scandal that was centring round a prominent society beauty, while another man began to be very boring about old china. At his opening words, however, it was decided to go upstairs and dance, and the bore was cut short in the middle of a sentence.

A few of the women were not dancing, but were sitting about in a corner watching the others. The Vicar at once made his way towards them, and began to keep up his reputation as being one of the most amusing men in London.

He was serious, witty, and intimate in turn, and they would have kept him there all the evening had not the Duchess finally come to the rescue and commanded him to dance.

He did his duty with the few important people, and then his eye wandered in search of the girl in pink. He was a beautiful dancer, and though a keen follower of all the latest steps he knew that he was at his best when waltzing. There was something about the lilting time and the wail of the violin that appealed to him. He knew that all eyes were upon them as they swayed in the centre of the room. He could imagine their remarks: 'What a lovely couple they make.'

Something of the kind was sure to be said. The Duchess was watching them from the doorway. Glorious woman, Norah, quite unique in many ways. She knew life, if anybody did; he could remember conversations with her – other things too – oh! yes, theirs had been a remarkable friendship. This child was as light as a feather. As they side-stepped in a corner he fancied that she leant a little against him. Delightful creature! He pressed her hand ever so slightly, and began to hum the tune under his breath.

Soon after midnight the Vicar left.

He did not believe in keeping late hours, they tired his brain and spoilt his temper.

However, he had enjoyed his evening.

The little girl had been very pretty, and amusing into the bargain; he flattered himself that he had made a very definite impression.

She was coming to St Swithin's anyway.

As he sank into bed he remembered with relief that the Curate was taking Low Mass at eight the following morning instead of him.

His prayers said, his sins of the day acknowledged, he fell asleep in a state of grace.

The next day, when he rose and went down into his study, it occurred to him that he had not prepared his sermon.

He glanced through the Sunday paper at random, in the hope of finding an inspiration.

There were two paragraphs that caught his attention, and disturbed him.

One was the copy of an article from a Socialist newspaper, attacking the smart society women, declaring them to be mere expensive ornaments who had never done a day's work in their lives, and who generally lived in idleness, immorality, and vice.

The other was shorter, and ran thus:

'The body of a young girl that was taken from Regent's Park Canal last night has been identified as that of a Miss Mary Williams, of 32 Clifton Road, St John's Wood, by her sister, Mrs Datchett, who had become alarmed at the girl's absence. It is believed that she stumbled in the dark and fell in, when walking home, and was instantly drowned. The inquest will be held on Tuesday.'

The Vicar stood silent for a while, his face white with emotion, his eyes gleaming.

'But this is monstrously unjust!' he cried aloud. He was thinking of the Socialist article.

St Swithin's was always packed for eleven-o'clock Mass on Sunday mornings.

Most people had their own pews, and those who had not, generally found it difficult to get a seat at all. Large queues began to form about twenty-to-eleven.

The singing of course was famous, and musicians would go for the anthem alone.

Upon entering the church one was aware of the pleasant drugged atmosphere; a mixture of heavy-scented flowers and waves of incense filled the air. Then the organ would start, a deep sensuous throb, soft and low, whose sound would gradually swell louder until the plaintive notes echoed through the church, and then lost themselves in a dim, hushed whispering among the rafters in the roof. The sweet voices of the choirboys quavered, immeasurably high, amid the chanting of the tenors.

Then the Vicar would stand before the altar, a far-away, impressive figure in his vestments, guarded by a little crowd of boys in red, who bowed before him and shook incense in his face.

It was in his capacity of priest that he really found himself. He felt that he was a shepherd of souls, a saviour of humanity.

The vast mass of people in the congregation were listening to his voice, thirsting for the consolation that he would give them.

The Mass was a drama of which he was the chief actor. Each prayer was a speech in which he had learnt to put the fullest amount of expression, a depth of colour, a world of significance.

The choir and organ served but as complements to his own voice. Thus in the call to Confession, when he said the words, 'Ye that do truly and earnestly repent you of your sins,' his voice was that of a judge, stern and merciless, but who was himself stainless.

And with what compassion he faced the congregation afterwards, with what pity he pronounced the Absolution! The people would rise from their knees with the agreeable feeling that all was now well.

Of course he had favourite parts of the Mass.

The words 'It is very meet, right, and our bounden duty' were one of his best intonations, but he knew that his triumph, his moment of exaltation, and one that was waited for eagerly by his little band of followers, was 'Therefore with Angels and Archangels, and with all the company of Heaven, we laud and magnify Thy Glorious Name, evermore praising Thee, and saying: "Holy, Holy, Holy"' – the choirboys chimed in, swelling their voices to his.

This was great, this was magnificent.

To-day, however, victory was to come to him in the pulpit. He ascended the stairway with the light of battle in his eyes.

His sermon was indirectly a defence of those beautiful women who had been so ruthlessly attacked by the Socialist article.

His text was superb: 'Consider the lilies of the field, they toil not, neither do they spin.'

From his first words his listeners were held.

A large number of the accused were present before him; he felt rather than saw the warm colour of pleasure mount into their cheeks.

They all hoped that he was addressing each of them personally, and they inwardly registered the vow to include him among the list of their most personal friends.

He knew this, his triumph was complete.

Not a sound disturbed the full rich tones of that glorious voice, the very air was breathless.

The little curate sat with bowed head. The doctor had told him that his wife must go to Switzerland, her right lung was already seriously affected and unless she could enjoy the benefit of another climate he would not answer for her life. But Switzerland meant hundreds of pounds, how was he to afford that?

For a week he had not slept, his head was nearly splitting with the agony of thinking.

And he was overwhelmed with work at the moment, the Vicar had entrusted the whole business of the Bazaar in aid of Unfortunate Women into his hands. If only there was someone he could turn to . . .

He looked up, a subdued giggle drew his attention to the choirboys. They were playing noughts-and-crosses amongst themselves. He frowned at them, but they replied by staring rudely at his feet.

He flushed − he knew the soles of his shoes were through. Oblivious of them all, the Vicar continued his sermon. He was drawing to the end now, he was finishing in a blaze of unparalleled eloquence. A sea of faces gazed up at him, the eager tools of his ambition.

Mary Williams was dead, he had forgotten her . . . The people he knew were before him, they would repay him for his noble defence. Words of flattery, words of praise seethed through his mind. Almost dazed, he heard the torrent of sound pour from him.

He lost himself in the beauty of his own voice. At last he paused, he ended on a note of supreme victory. The world was his. With a final gesture he turned his triumphant head:

'And now to God the Father . . .'

A Difference in Temperament

He leant against the mantelpiece, nervously jingling the change in his pockets. He supposed there would be another scene. It was so unreasonable the way she minded him going out without her. She never seemed to realise that he just had to get away sometimes – for no particular reason, but because it gave him a sense of freedom. He loved to slam the front door behind him, and to walk along the street to a bus, swinging a stick. There was something about the feeling of being alone he could not explain to anyone, not even to her. The delicious sense of utter irresponsibility, of complete self-ishness. Not to have to look at his watch and remember, 'I promised to be back at four,' but at four to be doing something quite different that she would not know. The feeblest thing. Even driving in a taxi she had never seen; to have the sensation of leaning back and smoking a cigar-ette without turning his head and being aware of her beside him. He would come back in the evening and tell her about it; they would sit in front of the fire and laugh; but at least it would have been his afternoon – not theirs, but his alone.

This was what she resented, though; she wanted to share everything. She could never imagine doing things apart from him. She had an uncanny way of reading his thoughts, too. If he was thinking of something that had no connection with her, she would know it at once. Only she exaggerated it in her mind. She would immediately think he was bored with her, that he did not like her any more. It wasn't that, of course; it wasn't that at all. Naturally, he loved her more than anyone in the world; in fact, there literally did not exist anyone but her. Why did she not realise this and be thankful? Why must she chain him to her, his mind, his body, his soul, without allowing the smallest part in him to stray, even for a little distance? She should understand that he would never go far, he would never go out of her sight – metaphorically; but surely just to the top of that hill, to see what was on the other side. No, even this she must share with him.

'Don't you see,' she would explain, 'that when I see anything or do anything there is no joy in keeping it to myself? I want to give everything to you. If I am alone and I see a picture that I love, or I read some passage from a book, I think to myself there is no meaning in this unless he knows it too. You are such a part of me that to stand alone leaves me dumb, without speech, without eyes. A tree with hatched branches, like someone with no hands. Life is valueless unless I can share everything with you – beauty, ugliness, pain. There must be no shadows between us, no quiet corners in our hearts.'

Funny! – yes, he saw what she meant, but he could not feel like this. They were on different planes. In the universe they were two stars, she far higher, burning with a steady light, but he flickering, unsteadily, always a little ahead – and in the end falling to earth, a momentary streak in the sky.

He turned to her abruptly.

'I guess I'd better go and have lunch in Town to-day,

58

after all. I promised that chap I'd see him again before he leaves, and I don't want to offend him. I'll be back early, of course.' He smiled a shade too sincerely.

She looked up from the letter she was writing. 'I thought you had arranged everything the last time you were together?'

'Yes – more or less. But I feel I ought to see him again, just once. It's a good opportunity to-day, don't you think? I mean, we weren't going to have done anything; you're busy.' He spoke easily, naturally, as if there was no question of her minding.

She was not deceived, though, not for a moment. Why was he never frank with her? Why not admit that he was no longer content to be with her, but must go out and seek any sort of distraction? It was his reticence that hurt her, his refusal to speak the truth. Like a wounded animal she spread out her claws to protect herself.

'You enjoy his company so much, when you have only known him for three weeks?' Her voice was hard and metallic.

He knew this voice. 'Darling, don't be ridiculous. You know I don't care a damn whether I see this fellow or not.'

'Why do you go, then?'

There was no argument to this. He yawned self-consciously and avoided her eyes.

She waited without saying a word. He pretended to lose his temper.

'I've told you I don't want to offend him. It's a bit thick; there's always this same old argument whenever I go out. Good God, it's only for a few hours! If you had your way you'd leave me without a friend in the world. You seem to be jealous if I speak to a dog.'

Jealous! She laughed contemptuously. He had misunderstood her again. As if she could possibly be jealous of the people he knew. It would be different if there was someone worth while. But this careless, selfish way he left her for anyone, for some creature he might not even see again! She despised the weak manner in which he shifted responsibility from himself.

'Go then,' she said, shrugging her shoulders, 'since it pains you to hurt a comparative stranger. I'm glad you've let me know. I shall remember in future. Perhaps you've forgotten that last Monday you promised this sort of thing would never happen again. I realise now that I can't depend on you at all. I've been making rather a fool of myself over you, haven't I? Well, aren't you going?'

Her eyes were cold. She had wrapped herself in a sheet of armour.

He turned his back and looked out of the window.

'Charming little scene for nothing at all,' he laughed lightly. 'It's pleasant, isn't it, living like this? Makes such an attractive atmosphere in the house. Scarcely a day passes without some sort of discussion, does it?' He rocked backwards and forwards on his heels, whistling a tune. He knew that every word tore at her like a knife. He was pleased. He wanted to hurt her. He didn't care.

She sat quite still, pretending to do accounts on a piece of paper. Calmly, dispassionately, she wondered why she loved him. His cruel, selfish nature, the way he took everything from her and gave nothing in return. If he would only realise that the smallest touch of recognition from him, the faintest sign that he would give up something unimportant for her sake, would send a flood of warmth to her heart. He did nothing. She felt herself drawing farther away from him, a lonely figure in an imaginary train. A grey shadow in a world of shadows. There was no one even to wave good-bye.

He watched her out of the tail of his eye. Why must she always parade her suffering before him? Not openly, not something that he could get hold of and flaunt in her face, but quietly, with the resignation of a martyr. A tear ran down her cheek and fell on to the blotting paper. Oh! hell – he wasn't going to stand for it. It was damn selfish of her, spoiling his day.

'Look here,' he started, as if nothing had happened, 'it's too late to put the whole thing off now. If you'd said something earlier, naturally I'd have done so. I won't be long, I promise. I'll be back soon after lunch.'

Surely this was a compromise. He was going out of his way to be nice to her. He waited to see how she would take it.

'Don't forget your coat, there's a bitter east wind,' she told him, and went on writing.

He hesitated a moment, wondering what to do. Did that mean everything was all right? No, he knew her too well. She would suffer the tortures of the damned until he returned. She would imagine every sort of accident. She would bottle up this scene in her mind, making more out of it than there had been. Why didn't he chuck away this footling lunch and stop with her? He didn't want to go now at all. He never had, really, all the time.

Another tear fell on to the blotting paper.

'Shall I not go after all? he suggested weakly, pretending not to notice the tear.

She made a movement of impatience. Did he think she was to be won as easily as this? He was trying to save himself. He was anxious to make up to her, to kiss and be friends like a child, and then forget all about it until the same thing happened again. Did he really want to stay with her? She gave him one more chance.

'Do just as you think best. Don't attempt to stay unless you feel like it.' Her voice was cool, impersonal.

Damn it all, she might show some sort of emotion. He had offered to stop, and this was how she took it. No, he didn't see why he should be always giving in to her. What a bore everything was. Why couldn't they live in peace? It was all her fault.

'Perhaps I'd better go, it looks rather rude,' he said carelessly, and strolled from the room, banging the door on purpose. He wouldn't bother to put on his coat, it would serve her right if he caught pneumonia. He had a vision of himself, stretched on a bed, coughing and gasping for breath. She bending over him with an agony of fear in her eyes. She would fight for his life, but she would lose. It would be too late. He could see her planting violets on his grave, a solitary figure in a grey cloak. What a ghastly tragedy. A lump came into his throat. He became quite emotional thinking of his own death. He would have to write a poem about this.

From behind the curtains she watched him walk to the end of the street. She was sure he had forgotten her already. She felt she did not care what he did any more. It was all over. She rang the bell and began to scold the maid for no reason.

He hated the lunch, the man was a bore – he couldn't even listen to what he was saying. He felt ill, too. His wish was probably coming true, and he was catching pneumonia.

What a God–forsaken fool he was to have come. There was no point in it at all. He had probably been and mucked up his life just for this. And all the while the fellow was rambling on about a whole lot of damned silly people he never wanted to see again. He'd cut everyone out of his life in future, nobody mattered but her. They'd leave this beastly country and go and live abroad. Perhaps when he went home he would find she had left him for good. There would be a note pinned on the desk. What would he do? He couldn't live without her. He'd commit suicide, he'd chuck himself into the river. Surely she loved him too much to do this. He could imagine the house blank and silent, the wardrobes empty of her dresses, the desk bare. Gone, leaving no address behind her. No, she would not do it, it was impossible. It was cruel, it would kill him. What on earth was this idiot jabbering about?

'I told her frankly I wasn't going to stand for it. I haven't the money for one thing, and, besides, I've got to consider my reputation. Don't you think I was right?'

'Oh! perfectly – absolutely.' He hadn't listened to a word. As if he cared about this fellow's hellish reputation.

'You know I must push off, I've got an appointment with my publisher,' he lied.

Somehow he managed to get away. What did it matter if he was rude? The man had ruined his life anyway. He leapt into a taxi. 'Drive like the devil!' he shouted. Stop, though, he suddenly had a longing to buy her something. The most priceless jewel – the most marvellous furs – anything. He would like to shower gifts at her feet. Perhaps there wasn't time for all this. It would have to be flowers after all. It was months since he had bought her flowers. How foul of him. He chose an azalea, an enormous one with pink waving buds. 'This will last a month or more if it's watered frequently,' said the woman.

'Will it really?' He became quite excited, he walked out of the shop clutching the pot in his arms. She would be pleased with this. A month! Pretty good value considering. The buds were small now, but they would open a little every day, they would get bigger, the plant would grow into a small bush. 'The symbol of my love,' he thought sentimentally.

Supposing she had gone, though, supposing she had killed herself? He would go mad, he would scatter the petals of the azalea over her body with a wild, despairing cry. Rather an effective scene for the last act, he must remember this. No, by God, he would never write another line again, he would dedicate the whole of his life to her, to her alone. Oh! how he was suffering. If she only knew what he was going through. His heart was bursting, it had never happened to anyone in the world before. What had he done that he should suffer so? He was certain there would be an ambulance outside the door, they would be carrying her limp form on a stretcher. He imagined himself leaping from the taxi, and covering her pale dead hand with kisses. 'My beloved – my beloved.' No, the street was empty. The house seemed unchanged. He paid the taxi and opened the front door – silently, like a thief. He crept upstairs, and listened outside her room. He heard her move. Thank God! Nothing had happened then. He wanted to shout for joy. He burst open the door, a fatuous smile on his face.

Poor darling, had she been writing letters all day? Her face was white and strained. Why on earth was she looking so unhappy? Wasn't she pleased to see him back?

64

'Look,' he stammered foolishly, 'I've bought you an azalea.'

She did not smile, she scarcely noticed the flower. 'Thank you,' she said in a dull voice. How inevitable of him. How unfeeling and unintelligent. Would he never understand her? Did he think he could just go off and enjoy himself after having broken her heart, and then bring back this plant as a peace offering? She could picture him saying to himself. 'Oh! I've only got to buy her a flower, and then kiss her, she'll forget all about this morning.'

If only it was as easy as that. His attitude wounded her, distressed her beyond measure. He had no heart, no delicacy of thought.

'Don't you like it?' he asked her, like a spoilt child.

Why had he bought the beastly thing? His agony at lunch, his terrible impatience in the taxi, meant nothing to her. Everything was a failure. The azalea looked foolish and conceited in its big pot. It seemed quite different in the shop. Now it mocked him, the colour was vulgar, much too pink. It was a hideous type of flower altogether. It didn't even smell. He wanted to crash it to the ground.

'Are you going to make a habit of this in future – a reminder for each time you hurt me?' she asked him.

She loathed herself, she hated her words, she longed to say something entirely different. The atmosphere was terrible. Why couldn't they be themselves again? He had only to make the first move. But her speech stung him, she insisted on ignoring every word he said.

'My God,' he shouted, 'there'll never be another time. I'm finished with the whole damned business, finished. Do you understand?'

He left the room, and went out of the house. The door slammed behind him.

'But that's not what I meant,' he thought, 'that's not what I meant at all.'

Frustration

After he had been engaged to her for seven years he felt that it was impossible to wait for her any longer. Human endurance had been tested to the limit. For seven years he had held her hand by the stile in the field, and it was beginning to pall at last.

It seemed to him that there must be more in life than these things.

He admitted that time had been when the simple fact of looking at her from a distance had ensured him weeks of fever and excitement, when the mere process of brushing against her on a tennis court had caused a state of nervous prostration.

Such follies belonged to the distant past. He was twenty-four now instead of eighteen. In the irony of his soul he wondered what Napoleon would have done if someone had offered him a box of tin soldiers; it occurred to him that Suzanne Lenglen in her day would have protested had she been compelled to play battledore and shuttlecock.

He was earnest, he was desperate, he was very much in love.

Saying good-night to her at half-past nine in the evening was a modern equivalent to the appalling tortures of the Spanish Inquisition. At these moments his legs twisted themselves inside out, his fingers clutched at the air, and his tongue got caught up in his uvula.

A low moaning noise rose in his throat, and he wanted to creep up a wall. Marriage seemed to be the one solution . . . Scarlet in the face, his hands clenched and his jaw set, he made his declaration to her father.

'Sir,' he began, 'I can't stand this any longer; I must get married.'

The father looked him up and down.

'I can well believe it,' he said; 'but it has got nothing to do with me. Personally, for a boy of your type, I put my faith in long engagements. You've been engaged for seven years. Why not draw up a contract for another seven?'

'Sir — we can't wait any longer. When we look at each other, we feel—'

The older man interrupted him brutally.

'I'm not at all interested in what you feel. Can you support a wife?'

'No — yes — at least. I will find a job.'

'Is there anything you can do?'

'I can tinker about with cars.'

'I see. Is that enough to make her happy?'

'I sort of . . .'

'You expect to make a girl happy when you've no money, no job, no qualifications, and the only thing you know how to handle is a spanner.'

'Sir, I—'

'Splendid. I'll say no more. My daughter is twenty-four; she can do as she likes. I'll pay for your wedding; but neither of you get a penny from me afterwards. You can work. I have a feeling your marriage will be a success.'

'Sir, may I — can I — I . . .'

'Yes, you can clear out.'

★ ★ ★

The wedding was good, as weddings go. There were church bells, white dresses, veils, orange blossom, and the 'Voice that Breathed o'er Eden'.

The bridegroom tripped over his feet, fumbled with the ring, forgot his lines, and looked at his bride as though she were a lump of chocolate and he were a Pekinese.

There were champagne, speeches and tears; the afternoon ended up with a cloud of confetti and somebody's old shoe. The bride and bridegroom left with nothing but five pounds, a couple of suitcases and a borrowed Austin Seven.

Their one stick of furniture was a tent.

'My darling,' he told her, 'I cannot afford to take you to a seaside hotel, not even for a weekend. We must sleep under the stars.'

His bride was more practical than he.

'We will motor to London in a borrowed car,' she said, 'and there we will find rooms and a job. But I must have a honeymoon first. Let's spend it in the tent I used as a Girl Guide.'

It seemed to him that this was the most romantic idea that had ever penetrated the human mind.

He gurgled strangely and waved his hands.

'A pig-sty with you would be Paradise,' he said, 'but to think of you in a tent . . .'

'There will be a moon,' she sighed, 'and trees murmuring, and a brook rippling.'

'I will slay some animal for your breakfast,' he cried, his voice breaking, 'and we'll roast it over a roaring fire. You can wear the skin to protect you from the bitter cold.'

'Don't forget it's June,' she said quickly, 'and we shall only be on Berkhamstead Common.'

'How wonderful you are, darling!'

'Am I?'

The Austin Seven bumped along the country roads.

In the evening they came to a wild stretch of heath that could be no other than their destination.

'We must not pitch our tent too close to the road,' he said. 'I want to feel that I'm alone with you, miles from civilisation, with nothing around us but the tangled gorse.'

'How shall we ever get the car over the rough ground?' she asked.

'We will leave it near the road, and we'll strike inland towards those trees. I'll carry the tent on my back.'

'You look like a prehistoric man, passionate and savage,' she told him.

'I feel it, my darling.'

It was dark before they had found a suitable camping-ground, and the tent was hoisted with difficulty. It had a queer list to starboard, and looked like the relic of a past age.

'We are like nomads,' she said vaguely, her mouth full of potted meat. It was cold, and she wished she had a warmer coat.

'Isn't it wonderful?' he said, trying to break the neck of a ginger-beer bottle. He had forgotten the opener.

After supper they sat outside the flapping tent, waiting for the moon that never came. Large clouds scurried across the sky.

'Darling,' he whispered, 'to think we have waited seven years for this. At last we are alone together, really alone. I couldn't have waited any longer.'

'No, nor could I. Isn't this the most romantic thing that's ever happened?'

They sat for a few minutes more.

'I think I'll go in the tent,' she said.

She disappeared, and he stood outside, smoking a cigarette.

His legs shook and his hands trembled. 'This is the most beautiful moment in my life,' he thought.

A sudden gust of wind blew at his hair. There was a patter in the trees, and a large cloud, hovering overhead, seemed to burst swiftly and silently.

'Darling,' she called softly.

He tiptoed inside. Another gust of wind blew across the heath, followed by the sheeting rain.

Two minutes later the tent fell in.

The grey dawn crept into the sky. The battered remains of white canvas fluttered hideously in the wind, like the torn rags of some long-dead explorer. A young man hammered at the pegs with the undaunted perseverance of the very great.

His clothes were sodden, his shoes were pulp. His bride, crouched in the fork of a tree, watched him with dull eyes. At last he admitted defeat, and kneeling in the comparative shelter of a gorse bush, he kept up a monologue that sounded like a chapter from James Joyce.

And the rain fell and the wind blew. Once a still small voice spoke from the fork of a tree.

'Darling,' it said, 'I believe we'd have been happier at Bournemouth, after all.'

Two figures stood side by side on the edge of the London road.

'I tell you it was here we left the car,' he repeated for the twelfth time. 'I remember this patch of stones.'

'I'm sure it was further back,' she said; 'there was a broken tree stump.'

'Well – wherever it was, it's not there now. It's been stolen; that's all.'

There was a sharp note of irritation in his voice. It is not every man who spends his wedding night in a gorse bush. And now the car was gone, and in it their two suitcases – nothing remained to them but the clothes they wore.

'Perhaps,' she suggested, 'this is a calamity that has been sent to test us.'

He said so-and-so, and so-and-so.

She looked about her vaguely.

'I don't see how they would help us,' she told him. 'Besides, I don't see any. No, darling, the only thing to do is to smile and be brave. After all, we have each other.'

'Darling, forgive me,' he said.

Hand in hand, they wandered along the road.

Hope springs eternal in the human breast . . .

They walked for hours, but in the wrong direction. They found themselves in Tring. They had lunch and walked again; they found themselves in Watford.

They caught buses, they caught trains; they found themselves in London.

It was nine in the evening once more. The day had passed slowly, horribly, yet with a subtle swiftness.

As children lost in a wood, they wandered up and down the Euston Road. Shabby, rain-bespattered and unwashed, they looked like the remnant of a hunger strike march.

Suddenly her shoe button burst. Stifling a groan, she bent her weary back to fix the strap.

As she did so, her wedding ring slipped off her finger and rolled into a drain . . .

They stood on the doorstep of a lodging-house.

'My wife and I want a room for the night,' he said. 'We camped out yesterday, and then our car was stolen, and so was our luggage.'

The woman glanced at the girl's left hand.

'My wife lost her ring, too,' he added.

The woman sniffed and shrugged her shoulders.

'You seem to have lost a good many things.'

'We are telling the truth,' he said coldly.

'I don't believe a word of your story,' answered the woman, 'but I won't turn you out this time of night.'

Meekly they followed her upstairs.

'The lady can have this room, and the gentleman the one at the end of the passage. This is a respectable house, and I'm a respectable woman.'

She frowned down at them, her arms akimbo.

'And I'm a very light sleeper.'

There seemed no more to be said.

She turned and left them in the passage.

'Good heavens! Have I got to creep like a thief to my own wife?' he whispered fiercely.

'Hush! she may hear,' she whispered back.

'Darling,' he said, 'you go to your room and wait for me. I'll pretend to go to mine, and then I'll come along to yours.'

'Supposing the boards creak?'

'I'll risk it. Darling, I love you.'

'So do I.'

He began to undress in his own room. The lodgings

73

might be uncomfortable, but they were better than a gorse bush.

What an appalling day it had been! But she had behaved marvellously. Any other girl would have gone home to her family.

To think he had waited for her seven years . . .

He opened the window, and as he did so the door of his own room slammed.

There was a noise of something falling on to the floor. He turned, and saw that the handle of the door had slipped off into the passage outside, while the useless knob lay at his feet . . .

The next morning he bought her a wedding ring at Woolworth's.

They moved to lodgings where the landlady was deaf, and where the door of the room bolted and double-locked.

It seemed to them that the world was theirs. The only trouble was that they had no money.

He left her alone while he looked for a job, and as soon as his back was turned she crept away to an agency. They must both work if they wished to live in comfort together.

How wonderful their life would be – the quiet suppers, the long evenings . . .

And, later, children playing about the floor.

They met at half-past six, he with his jaw set, a feverish glint in his eye.

'Darling, I've got a job,' he said.

'How splendid!'

'It's all I could get, but it's better than nothing. Anyway, we'll have to-morrow in the day-time, all to-morrow.'

'Oh! no,' she told him. 'I've got a job, too. I'm a daily

companion to a lady in Golders Green. My hours are from nine until seven.'

He stared at her as one who has heard sentence of death.

'You don't mean what you're saying!'

'Why! Whatever's the matter?'

'My hours are just the reverse. From seven until nine.'

'What do you mean?'

'Darling, I'm a night porter at a bank in Acton.'

Piccadilly

She sat on the edge of a chair swinging her legs. Her frock of black satin was too tight for her, and too short; as she tilted on her chair the dress rose above her knees, and I could see the beginning of a ladder in her stocking, hastily mended, the thread jumbled in a knot. Her hair was unnaturally light and over-waved; the vivid red of her lipstick, smudged and thick, toned badly against the pallor of her face dusted with a mauve powder. Her patent shoes were thin for walking, and cheap. The toes were too stumpy and the heels too high. She had thrown off her black coat, the collar and the cuffs of which boasted an imitation fur, and her hat, a minute piece of velvet worn at the back of her head, now lay at her feet. Around her throat was a necklace of scarlet beads that clashed with her mouth. Her face was thin, the skin drawn tightly across her cheekbones, and her eyes – silly doll's eyes, like blue china – stared sullenly in front of her.

Every now and then she puffed at a cigarette, pursing up her lips as a child would do, vainly attempting smoke rings, playing at bravado. She had sprinkled herself freely with scent, but even so it could not altogether hide the smell peculiar to one whose skin is rarely washed, whose clothes are seldom cleaned, whose body is under-nourished. She looked at me under her lashes, and then shrugged her shoulders, throwing aside her cigarette, forcing a smile that went ill with her appearance, that belonged to someone who must have been dead a long while. Then she began to talk at last, her voice hard and metallic, realising that I was not a man but a dummy thing without feeling, a note-book in my hand. 'Newspaper boy, that's it, is it?' she said. 'You've got to earn your living the same as I have. It's a dirty job, isn't it? When some fellow has left his wife for a new girl your boss sends you round to nose out where it was done and who with. Or else a kid is run over by a tram, and you call on the mother to hear how much blood he spilt. I guess you're popular all right in homes where things have gone wrong. I guess it gives you a sort of pleasure, doesn't it, to poke your fingers into people's lives? You'd think there was trouble enough without a boy like you trampling with heavy feet on something that ought to be kept dark and secret.

'What's it all for, can you tell me? So that Mr Smith can get a thrill to himself thinking, "I might have been that chap – unfaithful," so that Mrs Smith can wonder, "Might have happened to my kid?" No – I'm not clever, I'm not wise. But I kind of get time for thinking things now and again. Well, what do you want me to tell you? I've no secrets, not these days. I don't know anyone that's been murdered, nor run over, nor left sudden, nor waiting for a baby. I haven't any friends to speak of. I rub along better on my own. You know – I find the talk of other people silly. Seems as though whatever they say it wouldn't make a pennyworth of change if they'd left it all unsaid. The weather now – ah! that's different if you like. Weather means a lot to me. You understand that, don't you? I hate the rain – I can't afford to have it rain. And I hate the fog – I hate the winter – they're bad times for me. But for

78

Lady Stuck-up in her fur coat and her car, it doesn't hurt her. She's all right. And Miss Prim selling stockings behind a counter, she's all right. Half the world don't worry when it rains.

'But me, looking out of this window and seeing the sky like a dripping bucket, and saying to myself, "Will it stop before night?" and "Will my shoes let in the wet again?" Yes, and the chap who sells sunshades – *we* worry. Come on, tell me it takes all sorts to make a world. They told me that in school. I don't know why you want to ask me questions. Is it that you're doing a piece in your paper called "Confessions of the Great"? I've seen that sort of stuff before. "How I became an Actress", by Florrie Flapdoodle, or "My First Step Towards the Church", by the Archbishop of Bunk. You want to pry into the lives of humble people like myself. "As a Kid I loved handling Corpses," said the Undertaker. Is that it? So you want me to give it you, hot and strong, straight from the shoulder.

'Listen, you funny little fellow with your notebook and your inky fingers. I'll tell you a story. Maybe it's true, maybe it isn't. You can make what you like out of it and print it in big letters in the "Sunday Muck": "What Led to My Entering the Profession", by Mazie.'

You see, in a kind of way, everything happened because of superstition. I've always been mad for superstition. Walking under ladders, crossing my salt, bowing to the moon, hunting up passages in the Bible. Even now it's the same. Every morning I open my Bible to see if it's going to be my lucky day. Laughing at me? I tell you I'm serious. A girl I knew found 'God shall send a pestilence unto ye,' and in a fortnight she had it. She didn't laugh.

All she knew was that it didn't come from God . . . We're like that, every one of us. Believing in legends, believing in symbols, believing in signs – the only things we don't believe in are fairies.

Listen – if I wasn't superstitious I'd be a housemaid now in Park Lane. It's a fact. I'd be wearing a cap and an apron. I'd be emptying the slops of some overfed old countess. I'd be meeting my boy Thursday night under a lamp-post and going to a picture house for one-and-three-penny-worth of cuddle. And, look at me – I'm free, I don't owe anything to no one, I belong to myself. Haven't I got a room of my own? Once I was a kid that didn't know a thing. I went into service straight from the Soldiers' Orphan Home. A kitchenmaid in Kensington, that was me. No, I hadn't got any relations. Never knew my parents. The fellow who met my mother on a foggy night must have worn a uniform, else I wouldn't have been sent to the Soldiers' Orphan Home. I was happy because I was ignorant. I used to scrub myself every day with soap and wear flannel next the skin. I didn't know any better. I thought if I rose from under-housemaid to upper maybe I'd save enough at fifty to live quiet in the country.

I wanted to marry, too. I thought if you kissed a boy he took you straight away to church. Then I met Jim. Jim didn't take me to church nor did he kiss me much, but he taught me a whole lot of things housemaids don't need to know. I felt for Jim what girls in books feel for the fellow on the cover. You know, he has big eyes and curly hair. Jim's hair was straight and he had a cast in one eye, but I didn't worry. I don't know if there's a name for it – what Jim and I had. In the pictures they call it Love. In the newspapers they call it an Offence. I didn't call it

80

nothing, but it seemed all right to me. I had a pain in my heart when he wasn't there. I'd wait around in the rain; I wouldn't work proper. I thought maybe he'd leave me if I didn't look nice. So I gave up washing and bought some scent and powder, and he said I was fine. He used to say to me, 'Look here, Mazie, service isn't any good to you. You're too smart.' 'Why,' I'd tell him, 'I can't do anything else.' 'Of course you can,' he'd say, 'there's heaps of things you could do. Service is drab. It doesn't lead you no-where.' When I told him maybe one day I'd get to upper housemaid he laughed.

'Are you going to waste your days planning what'll come to you when you're fifty?' he said. 'I thought you'd got more sense.'

I told him he was mean, but I thought about it all the same. I thought maybe he'd look down on me if I stayed in service. 'If I leave my place you'll have to find me a job,' I said. He looked queer then, he didn't say much, but next time we went together he petted me so I felt I'd do anything he wanted as long as I didn't have to lose him. 'I treat you all right, don't I?' he said. 'How do you think I earn money to take you out and give you good times?'

'I don't know. You work, don't you?'

'Yes, I work, Mazie, but not the way you mean.'

'Well, tell me,' I said.

Then he laughed, slyly, winking at me. 'Look at this,' he said, and he took a necklace out of his pocket and jingled it up and down before my eyes.

'Where'd you find that?' I asked him.

'Took it off an old lady,' he said.

Then I understood. Jim was a thief. I was scared. I cried, I said I wouldn't have any more to do with him. I was honest, I said. 'All right,' he laughed, and went off, not coming near me for three weeks.

That taught me. I saw I couldn't do without him. I wrote him he could steal the Crown Jewels if he liked, as long as he took me back. I thought p'raps I could reform him and one day I'd save enough money to keep him and buy a little house in the country. I gave in my notice to the lady in Kensington. I saw an advertisement in a paper for an under-housemaid in a place in Park Lane.

I showed it to Jim. 'That's me,' I said. He laughed. 'You can't do that,' he said. 'You come and get rich my way.'

I put the advertisement in my bag.

'I'm going to answer it today,' I told him.

'We'll see,' he said.

He said he'd come with me. We went to the Underground and booked to Down Street. I was fussed and worried, I wondered if I was doing the right thing – answering that advertisement.

'Look here,' said Jim, 'let's make a bargain. Either you go to Park Lane or you come and live with me, work with me. You can't do both; quick now, decide.' He said this as we got into the train. I shut my eyes tight. I thought, 'If only there could be a sign to tell me what to do.' Then I opened my eyes, I glanced at the platform as the train carried us away. Suddenly I saw the words flash up at me in lights on a board: 'Passing Down Street.'

Then I said aloud to Jim, 'All right. I'll come to you.'

Yes, you can call it superstition. Each thing has happened to me in that way. In the Underground, too. Funny, isn't it? Never up in the air, never up in the world. Always below, beneath the ground. I was with Jim for about six months. He trained me so I could steal women's handbags without their noticing. It was quite easy. I was expert after a time.

We worked the Underground. I got to know every station, every lift – all the network of passages. Sometimes it was exciting, and dangerous, making me want to laugh, but more often it was hell. Sometimes I'd tremble so I'd come over faint. 'Pull yourself together,' Jim would whisper, 'do you want to give us away?'

Sometimes he'd make me go alone. Then I'd be scared. It seemed as though everyone must be looking, and that I was there, all alone, no one near, nowhere to hide if things went wrong.

'You're not bold enough,' Jim told me, 'how d'you think we're ever going to get rich if you act timid the way you do? Handbags don't bring us in much unless you get a lucky haul. You've got to learn an' be more snappy. Most women nowadays wear bracelets. Why can't you have a try at them?' He'd always be worrying at me.

'Can't you lift a bracelet?' he'd say. He'd complain all the time. He was lazy now, he made me do the work.

One evening when I'd only lifted one bag the whole day he turned nasty. 'I'm coming out with you tonight,' he said, 'and we're going to get a bracelet.' I began to cry. 'I can't,' I said. 'I don't feel sure of my fingers.'

'You'll do as I tell you or I'm finished with you,' he said.

We started to work the Central London line shortly after eleven. We counted on getting the after-theatre crowd. It was at Oxford Circus he saw the old lady in the fur coat walk to the booking office. She booked to Lancaster Gate. Jim nudged me, pointed to her hands.

She wore a large ring on her little finger. It looked valuable, too. We also booked to Lancaster Gate. I was

83

trembling all over, and my hands were slippery with sweat. 'I can't do it,' I whispered. 'I can't do it.' He held my arm so tight I nearly screamed. We didn't sit next to her in the carriage. We were in another part of the train.

When we got out at Lancaster Gate she was walking up the platform. There were few people about, I saw it was going to be difficult. There wouldn't be the excuse of jostling in a crowd.

She was in evening dress. It was long at the back. She couldn't manage it proper. I thought that perhaps if she tripped in some way . . . I brushed against her – she dropped her bag. We both groped for it on the floor. The bag opened and her powder-box and purse and odds and ends fell out in a mess. I talked loudly, fussing her, pretending to help, bumping her against the wall – but I had the ring. Then I left her, and ran on to catch the lift, Jim just behind me. 'Something is going to happen,' I thought, 'something is going to happen . . .' I felt I could see prison in front of me, and I couldn't escape. If the old lady missed her ring in the lift I was done for. I wondered if I had better turn back and get through to the other platform. I knew if I went up in that lift I was finished. And as though to prove it – as though there really was something true in superstition – I saw the notice: 'Stand clear of the Gates.'

I turned to Jim. 'I'm going back,' I said. He was rough, he shook my arm. 'Get in quick – you little fool,' he said. But he was scared, too. I could see the whites of his eyes. He pushed me inside the lift. I saw the old lady running along the passage waving her hand. 'I've been robbed,' she shouted, 'I've been robbed. Stop that girl.'

84

People turned to look at me. I tried to get to the other side of the lift, but it was barred. Then they began to crowd round me and to question me.

You don't want me to tell you about gaol, do you? You can squeeze that out of somebody else. There's plenty of ex-convicts who like to get into the newspapers. I've got nothing to say . . . Oh! Yes – they treated me kind. That's right, isn't it?

And a lady visited me once a week and asked me if I'd been a bad girl, and wouldn't I be happier with Jesus? I told her 'No,' I didn't care how dirty he'd been to me I'd go with Jim and no one else. That was true, too. Maybe he'd turned me down, but I was his girl. I only wanted to get clear of gaol to be with him again. He told me it was the same for him. He came and saw me once. You stand in a kind of place with bars around, and they let you talk to your friends. 'Why, Mazie,' he said. 'You know I didn't mean to get you in here, don't you?'

'That's all right – I haven't split,' I said.

'You aren't sore at me, Mazie, are you?' he said, 'it just happened that way, and it couldn't be helped. I tried to save my skin. You won't let on to them here we were working together, will you?' he said.

I told him he needn't worry.

'You're a sweet kid,' he told me, 'I'm fond of you. It's lonely without you.'

He didn't talk no more after that, and he went away. He never came back again neither. But somehow I pictured him waiting for me outside. I guessed he'd be helpless without me fiddling with his things and just being near him.

A man likes to have a girl around if it's only to treat her rough and swear at her, don't you think? It gives him a queer kind of comfort. And loving a girl makes a man forget to wonder why it was he was born.

I guess that's what it was like for Jim, anyway. So back in gaol I'd make plans of what we'd do when I was out again. I thought we'd have to lie low for a bit because of my coming from gaol. They keep a pretty sharp eye on you, so I was told by one of the girls. It's no use working your old game again until they've slacked off from watching you. I didn't want to land Jim into trouble either.

There was a kid in there with me who said she was going to go straight when she was out. She believed in the stuff that the visiting lady handed her. I was wise, though. 'You'll never be free of this,' I said, 'it clings like mud, don't you know that?'

'Oh! Mazie,' she said, crying, too – young she was – 'I wish you'd come with me, and we'd go out to the colonies together.'

'What? and be treated worse than a servant, and scrubbing floors, and people above you?' I said. 'I've had enough scrubbing inside here to last me a lifetime. When I get outside I'm going to live like a princess. I've got a boy waiting for me,' I said.

She was free before me. 'I'm going to Canada,' she said. 'I'm starting fresh.'

Funny thing – they put her with a clergyman's wife up in Bristol, and found out a month later she had started her old tricks again, so they gave her three years.

It just shows you, doesn't it?

I got out in the spring. They talked to me before I left about duty, and citizenship, and humanity, and God. They gave me some money, too. I went out and bought a pair of camiknickers trimmed with lace. I wanted Jim to find me smart. There never was a day like the day I came out. Blue sky and the sun, and people smiling for no reason. I felt like dancing, and screaming with laughter, and being looked at by fellows, and running away in a corner to cry at the same time.

I kept saying to myself, 'Soon I'll be seeing him, soon – soon.' I had myself kind of worked up. D'you see? He'd be somewhere around. I knew that. I'd only got to go and find him; he wouldn't be far.

So I looked up at the sky and talked like a baby. 'Here – you be off – you aren't any use to me,' and I went down into the Underground where I belonged.

I looked for him all day, and I was getting tired, and sore, too. I felt myself thinking, superstitious like – 'Maybe there'll be a sign soon to show me what's going to happen.' Yes, it was six o'clock, what they call the rush hour in the Underground. I guessed if Jim was still working he'd be busy at that time. I took a ticket at Bond Street. I had to stand nearly five minutes in a queue. I was hot, my clothes sticking to me, my hat at the back of my head.

I wanted to lie down and die . . .

And the crowd pushing into me, breathing down my neck, straining to get past me, to go their way. I got my feet on the moving stairway – I leaned against the rail. We were taken downwards, away from the light above, down into the Underground. And then I saw Jim. He was across the rail, on the other side, on the same staircase – but *coming up*. We drew nearer, we were level – and I called out to him, over the barrier that separated us: 'Jim – here I am – Jim.' He didn't look. He didn't speak. He heard me, but he didn't do anything. He seemed smarter, different and there was a girl with him – hanging on his arm. I

87

turned, I tried to push back, but there were people coming down behind me all the time and it wasn't any use. I called out to him once more – 'Jim – Jim.'

There wasn't anything I could do. I let the moving stair take me where it wanted – down – down. And he, the last I saw of him was a figure right at the very top, blotted against a girl – going out into the air.

She stretched across to a table and picked up a bottle of nail varnish.

'So that was my sign,' she said; 'he going up the stair-case and me going down. That's what you wanted to know, wasn't it? It'll make a pretty picture for your newspaper. Tell me, do they pay you well for this sort of thing?'

Still she tilted on the edge of her chair, swinging her legs.

'Aren't you satisfied yet? D'you like every single scrappy detail? You ask me why I didn't go back to being a servant? Because, little newspaper boy, servants can't have the things I want. Why didn't I go on being a thief? Because I was scared, and I had to have a job that was easy to do. Why did I choose, beyond anything else in the world, to be what I am? Is that what you want, to put it in headlines?' She laughed, she shrugged her shoulders, she was no longer the Mazie who had told her story, but the Mazie of the moment – ugly, older, hard, false, and without feeling.

She said: 'Because when I got to the bottom of that moving stairway I walked to a train, and I got out at a station, and I got in another train, and I got out at another station – and as I stood on the platform I prayed hard to God that He should give me a sign. And He did.'

She finished her nails. She dabbed her face with powder,

her lips with rouge. She pulled on her coat and her hat, she stood ready with her bag under her arm. She opened her mouth and laughed.

'What was the sign?' she said. 'Why, it came straight from God written big above my head, in letters of fire at the end of the platform – "Follow The Red Light For Piccadilly".'

Tame Cat

I t was difficult to believe that she had grown up at last. She had looked forward to this moment all her life, and now it had come. The little petty worries of childhood lay behind her for ever. No more French, no more hateful plodding round the Louvre, with Mademoiselle in charge, no more sitting at the round table in the *petit salon* – an English novel surreptitiously concealed behind the volume of history.

Already the life at the *pension* seemed dim and quite unreal. The child who cried herself to sleep because Mademoiselle had frowned was a stranger to her, a lost shadow. And the chatter of the girls, the little fierce intimacies of day to day, once so important, were now empty, nonsensical things scarce remembered. She was grown up. The wonderful things of life lay before her. To say what she liked, to go as she pleased, to stay at a dance until three in the morning, perhaps, and drink champagne. She might be seen home in a taxi by a young man who would want to kiss her (she would refuse, of course), and the next morning he would send her flowers. Oh! and there would be so many new friends, new things, and new faces. It would not be all dancing and theatres, of course; she knew that. Later on she must settle down seriously to her music; but just for a while she wanted to fill herself with this warm, happy flood of excitement, so new, so tremulous;

91

like the carefree flight of a butterfly, on a May morning, she would dance and she would sing.

'I'm grown up! I'm grown up!' The words sang in her ears, and the clatter of the train took the theme and thundered it loud, over and over again. 'I'm grown up! I'm grown up!'

She thought of the welcome that awaited her. Mummy, exquisitely dressed and more beautiful than ever, lovelier than she could ever hope to be, hugging her carelessly and rumpling her hair, 'Darling, you're like a fat puppy – go away and play.' But Mummy would not be able to say that this time, because she had grown so slim since last holidays, and then, having her hair waterwaved had made such a difference to the shape of her face. The new dress, too, and the touch of colour on her lips. Mummy would be proud of her at last. What fun they would have, going about together everywhere, doing the same things, meeting the same people! This was, perhaps, the thing to which she had looked forward most in her life – being with Mummy. They would be such companions. Darling Mummy was so generous, so hopelessly extravagant; she really needed someone to look after her. They would be like sisters.

Of course, there was Uncle John . . . She could not remember the time when there had not been Uncle John. He was not really any relation at all, but it was just the same as though he were. It was at Frinton they had met him first, she believed, when she was a tiny girl, bathing with Mummy in shallow water; but it was all so very long ago. Uncle John had been part of the household now for years. He was useful to Mummy in a hundred ways. It was Uncle John who answered letters for Mummy and argued with tradesmen when the bills were too heavy. It was Uncle John who saw to the tickets on journeys and booked rooms at hotels. Although he did not actually live in the house, he was nearly always in to meals, and when he was not there for lunch or dinner, it meant that he had taken Mummy to a restaurant or to the theatre. It was Uncle John who had made Mummy buy so many new cars at different times, but of course he was a very good driver.

Yes, Uncle John was useful to Mummy, and rather a dear – quite old, though; well over forty. Poor old Uncle John! What was it that one of the girls at the *pension* had said about him when they had passed through Paris in the summer, on their way to Cannes? 'That your mother's tame cat?' What a good expression! Tame cat. Perhaps Uncle John was rather like a cat, a dear, harmless old tabby tom-cat, purring quietly in a corner, never showing his claws, lapping away peacefully at his saucer of milk. Well, he would carry their coats for them and take them to the theatre and act partner at dances – they were going to be so happy, she and Mummy and Uncle John.

And now she was getting almost too excited to sit still. The cold dark evening did not matter; the stuffy Pullman car did not matter. The train was drawing near to Victoria. Her heart was thumping, and a little pulse beat in her temple. The great, friendly roar of London, the rumble of buses, the yellow light of shops bursting with Christmas decorations – if this was being grown up, then she was younger than she had ever been in her life, young with a hope born of inexperience, a glow within her bright as the unseen paradise. Now was the supreme moment, never equalled and never surpassed, as the train drew into Victoria.

She stepped out on to the platform, eager, flushed, her eyes very bright and blue, her velvet beret on the side of her head. 'Mummy, Mummy, darling, I'm so happy, so terribly happy to be back!' But something had happened; something was wrong. Mummy was looking at her in astonishment, almost in dismay, and then as though she were angry, were afraid.

'Baby – what on earth . . .' she began, but her voice trailed off uncertainly, and then she laughed, a little too brightly, a little too gay. 'You've done something to yourself, haven't you?' and, changing abruptly to a hard, careless tone: 'I suppose you've got a mass of luggage. Go and cope with it, John. I'm freezing. I'll wait in the car.'

The girl watched her go, a little sick feeling of disappointment in her heart, and turned to the man who waited beside her, his hat in his hand, his eye on her face.

'Hullo, Uncle John!' But why must he stare like that, the old sleepy expression gone and a new one in its place, alert, beady, *queer*?

It was being so different from what she had expected. The breathless feeling of anticipation had fled, and in its place had come a horrid sense of staleness, almost of boredom. She felt lonely and shut within herself. It was something to do with Mummy. Mummy was not well; ever since she had come back from school Mummy had been cold, easily irritated, snappy with her.

And she herself had taken so much trouble to please Mummy. She had been extra careful about her appearance, worn the new dress that suited her, chatted and laughed with Mummy's friends as though she had been 'out' for years. They were charming to her, and made much of her, inviting her to dances, to week-ends, to house-parties, all the gaieties she had hoped for in the train. But now everything was spoilt, because Mummy was not pleased.

From the very beginning, Mummy had been cold to her. The first morning, when they had gone to buy the evening dress, Uncle John in attendance, as usual, and she had wanted the lovely peach velvet with the low back. 'My dear Baby, don't be such a little fool; it's years too old for you,' brushing her timid question aside. 'No, Louise,' to the attendant; 'something much more simple, in white'; and then, turning round to Uncle John in irritation: 'Well, what are you gaping at? I suppose you'd like to see the child dolled-up like a tart?'

She had never heard Mummy speak like that in her life before. Quickly, shamefully, she whispered: 'Yes, let me have the white; it looks very nice,' hating it in her heart: the band at the waist, the thick shoulder-straps, so school-girlish; but she would wear anything if it would change the expression on Mummy's face, so hard, with peeved lines at the corner of her mouth.

And then, when Mummy was not looking, Uncle John had whispered in her ear: 'It's a damned shame! You'd look lovely in the velvet, lovely,' smiling at her, patting her hand, as though they were allies, ranging himself on her side as it were, furtively, like an accomplice. 'If you want anything, come to me,' he had told her later that day, pulling her into a corner, glancing over his shoulder through the crack in the door. 'Don't worry your mother, just come along to me.' And for a moment she had felt like laughing, he was so much the tabby cat, sleek and well fed, purring slightly and arching his back. 'Thank you, Uncle John, you're a lamb,' she said, kissing him impulsively; when, to her surprise, he went dark red, hesitated a moment, then kissed her back. 'We're going to be friends, aren't we, Baby?' he said, squeezing her hand. 'But we always have been,' she answered, feeling, for the first time in her life, shy and uncomfortable, as though he were a stranger.

The days which should have been filled with joy and new interests passed slowly, like the old school holidays, and, for all the change, she might still be the child at the *pension*. Mummy made excuses for the many invitations they received. 'Later on, perhaps,' she would say vaguely, and then go off with Uncle John alone, leaving her to ring up a school friend and spend half a crown at the Plaza.

Christmas Day was spent with Granny in the country, as usual: a heavy mid-day lunch, followed by a walk in the rain in the afternoon; and Boxing Day was relieved by the Circus and a cousin to dinner. But after that the week stretched dully on until New Year's Eve. Surely nothing would happen to spoil that? Mummy's funny mood would leave her; Uncle John would be himself again. There was to be a big party at the Savoy; a party given entirely for her, when everyone would know she was grown up and a child no longer. Most passionately she prayed that it would be a success, this, her first party, and Mummy would be the old Mummy, careless and affectionate, proud of her daughter so like a younger sister; and she would wear her new dress, even if it were a little too full, a little too young. 'Please, God, let everything be all right,' she whispered at bed-time, rocking on her knees in a fervour of faith; and, going to the window, pulled aside the curtain, where bright in the sky a star shone, as she would shine, fairer than the others, on New Year's Eve.

Mummy went to bed early the night before the party. She had her dinner taken up to her on a tray. She felt tired, she said, worn out. She hoped she would be better by to-morrow, but, really, if she wasn't, the whole thing would have to be put off, even if it meant disappointing Baby. Better that than the whole house down with 'flu. Her throat was sore, and it might easily be 'flu. One could not be too careful, this time of the year. Her daughter kissed her good-night and wandered, disconsolate, into the drawing-room.

She sat down at the piano and played softly, for fear of disturbing Mummy. It couldn't be going to be 'flu, not suddenly like this, the night before the party. Sometimes she wondered if Mummy behaved like this on purpose, and, for some queer, unknown reason, did not want her to be happy. And then the door opened, and Uncle John came into the room. He looked flushed and rather excited; he beckoned to her in a mysterious manner.

'Come on,' he said, 'be a sport. When the cat's away . . .'

Had he been to a cocktail party, and drunk one too many? Poor Uncle John. 'What's the matter?' she said. 'Mummy's in bed, you know; she's not well.'

'Of course I know,' he said. 'That's why I'm here. Going to take you out to dinner.'

For a moment she stared at him in wonder, and then she smiled. Why, it really was rather sweet of him to think of her all alone. He had guessed her Christmas had been a failure, and now he had called for her, in evening dress and everything, because he was sorry for her. Besides, it must be so boring for him, when there were probably heaps of people he could go out with, to put up with her chatter.

97

'Where shall we go?' she asked, suddenly happy, suddenly excited; and 'Can I put on my new dress?' and 'Could we go to a theatre?'

She ran upstairs, remembering just in time to tiptoe past Mummy's door. Really, she looked rather nice, she thought, glancing at herself in the long looking-glass, and with a shaky hand she put just a little too much lipstick on her mouth. Uncle John, more of a tabby-cat than ever, waited for her in the hall. He positively purred in satisfaction, tugging at his little moustache.

'You monkey!' he said. 'They've taught you a thing or two in Paris, haven't they?' And this was what he kept hinting all the evening, suggesting she knew so much, egging her on to make confessions to him.

'But, honestly, we didn't go anywhere,' she told him for the tenth time. 'It was lessons and lectures all the time.'

'Oh, don't tell me . . .' he retorted, filling her glass. 'I can see by your eyes, you're entirely changed.'

How silly he was, grinning away like the Cheshire Cat in *Alice*! Should she tell him the Tame Cat story? But perhaps it would hurt him, and he was really being so kind, such a dear, and giving her the happiest evening since she had been home.

The champagne made her giggle, made her chatter too much, but he did not seem to mind. He laughed loudly, whatever she said; and 'I know, I understand,' he kept saying. 'A pretty girl like you wants to have a good time, and why not? A girl can do as she likes these days. You know that, don't you, Baby? I'll see to it, too, in spite of—' But he did not go on with his sentence; he pulled himself up short with a jerk, avoiding her eye.

It seemed to her that everyone was smiling at her as

98

they left the restaurant. They knew she was Mummy's daughter; they stopped Uncle John; they asked to be introduced.

'I remember you as a little girl. How lovely you've grown!' Rather embarrassing and overwhelming, perhaps, but nice of them, and kind.

'Enjoying yourself?' asked Uncle John, and she smiled back at him, flushed, excited.

'I'm having a lovely evening. If only Mummy were here!'

He looked at her foolishly, his mouth open, his head slightly on one side. Then he guessed she must be joking. He burst into a loud cackle of laughter.

'I say, you're a bit thick for a youngster; you really are!'

But she was not listening to him; she was looking around her, her eyes dancing, drinking in the new sights and sounds, already in her mind miles away from him and alone with somebody else, somebody new, somebody young. And what fun it was to sit in the third row of the stalls, and go out during the intervals and smoke a cigarette, when the last time she had been to the theatre it was in a cramped *loge* with Mademoiselle and three girls, to see *L'Avare*, and they had actually eaten chocolates! How odious, how childish! But in this play there was music, there was dancing, there was a golden-haired girl who pirouetted against a background of stars; there was a slim, dark boy who sang a song to the sea; and through it all a mad, jigging tune was whispered on a violin, inserting itself in the memory, persistent, unforgettable.

Oh, dear! she was feeling it all too deeply, she told herself; it couldn't last – so much beauty and romance. How glad she was that the couple came together at the end, after that bitter quarrel in the second act! And now it was 'God Save the King', mournful, throbbing. A sob rose in her throat, and she thought how easily she could die for her country; but in a minute it was over, forgotten. They were crowding out of the theatre into a taxi, pushing through the Piccadilly traffic all ablaze with electric signs and flashes, stopping with a jerk as the purple-uniformed commissionaire of the night club opened the door.

What was Uncle John muttering? Something about it being damn slow after Paris? How obstinate he was! Almost a bore. It was his age, she supposed. For she was tingling all over with impatience as the band struck up the tune that had been singing in her head all evening, and it seemed as though a hundred faces shone up at her from the crowded tables – bare arms, silver dresses, dark eyes, white shirt-fronts; so much bustle and clatter and laughter. Now they were dancing at last, the lights a little dim; she turning her face to right and to left, searching the faces of the passing couples.

And a boy smiled at her over his partner's shoulder, infectious, gay. She had to smile back. Surely they were both thinking the same thing. 'Why aren't we dancing together?' They could not drag their eyes away from each other; he followed with his partner behind her, lost in a dream. She never even heard Uncle John whisper in her ear: 'You know, we'll have to be damn careful, Baby – if she suspects there's anything between us . . .'

Of course, it had to come to an end. She did not know if it was three or four o'clock – she had lost all count of time, and she could have gone on dancing for ever. She stood in the drawing-room at home, saying good-night to him, too full and happy to speak. He wondered why she was silent; he kept peering down at her anxiously. 'What's the matter? Are you angry with me? Disappointed?' Silly Uncle John! He seemed quite humble, and anxious to please; at times almost sentimental.

'You've given me the most wonderful evening I've ever had in my life,' she told him.

Suddenly a door closed overhead, and steps sounded on the landing. Uncle John started, went white, then turned and seized her by the shoulders. His expression had entirely changed. Gone were the sleek, smooth creases from nose to chin; gone was the bland smile, the light in the round, beady eyes. Into his face something furtive had crept, something creeping and sly; his mouth curved, his eyes half-shut. He looked like a cat, a sly, slinking tom-cat, crouching in its own shadow against a dark, damp wall.

'She's heard us,' he whispered. 'She's coming downstairs. Whatever happens, we've got to put her off the scent. She mustn't guess about us, d'you hear? We must lie like hell, invent some story. Keep quiet; leave it to me.'

She looked at him, bewildered.

'Why on earth should Mummy mind—?' she began. But he stopped her impatiently; his eyes towards the door.

'Don't pretend to be so damned innocent,' he said. 'You know perfectly well it's an appalling situation. Oh, my God! . . .' He turned away, fumbling with a cigarette, his hands trembling.

The girl heard her mother's voice outside the room.

'Is that you, John? What are you doing down here? I've had an awful evening. I couldn't sleep . . .'

She stood in the doorway and saw them both; the man puffing cigarette-smoke, watching her round the tail of his eye; and the girl clasping her childish pink evening bag, twisting it in her fingers.

Mummy had thrown a wrap over her nightgown, holding it across her loosely with one hand. Her face was a mask of powder, carelessly, too hurriedly applied. Lines dragged to her mouth, and her eyes were puffy. There was no trace of beauty at this moment. She was just a woman of middle-age who had slept badly. The girl noticed this at a glance, and felt ashamed for her, hating that anyone should see her so wan and haggard.

'Oh, Mummy, I am sorry! Have we woken you up?' she said.

There was silence for a moment, tense and frightening; and then Mummy laughed – a forced, horrible sound, her face as white as Uncle John's.

'So I was right all the time,' she said; 'it wasn't just my imagination – all those secret looks and whispering in corners. How long has it been going on for? Ever since you came back from Paris, or did it start last summer? You work quickly for a child of your age, don't you? You might at least have had the decency to go somewhere else, and not use my house.'

Uncle John broke in hurriedly, the words tumbling over themselves. 'My dear, I assure you . . . nothing wrong . . . ask Baby . . . begged me to take her out – sorry for the kid . . . wanted to stay with you . . . it never entered my head . . . absolutely absurd . . .' Little, short, jerky sentences, entirely unconvincing, sounding a string of lies even to the girl who stood at his side.

But the woman would not listen to him. She could not

102

leave her daughter alone. It was Baby who was false, who had lied, who had worked against her — the man was nothing, merely a shadow.

'How dare you!' she was saying. 'How dare you come back from Paris and behave like a cheap, third-rate girl off the streets? Directly you came home I guessed what you were trying to do: I could see it in your eyes. Oh, you worked quietly enough; you didn't make a show of it! You were determined to get him, though, weren't you? Nobody else would do. It had to be him. I've been told that's what girls of your age make for. They've got to have a man who belongs to somebody else. I suppose you think I'm going to share him . . . ?'

The girl did not answer. She could only stare back at her mother, physically sick with horror and shame, the realisation of what had happened branding itself in her mind. Mummy and Uncle John. Mummy and Uncle John at Frinton, ten, twelve years ago. Mummy and Uncle John in London, Paris, Cannes. All those years, buying tickets, driving cars, seeing the tradesmen, paying bills, all his meals in the house, day after day, night after night. Mummy and Uncle John.

That little, sleek, tubby man, with his small moustache, carrying their bags at stations, handing bread and butter at tea, answering the telephone, and keeping the engage-ment-book up to date; rubbing his hands together when he was pleased, smiling, obsequious, humble — Uncle John. She understood everything now. Mummy, her beauty gone, a frightened jealous woman, envious of her own youth; while he, smooth-tongued and deceitful, worked for a new alliance.

So being grown up was this: a sordid tissue of intimate

103

relationships, complicated and vile. No loveliness, no romance. She would have to live like this in her turn, be false, be hard, wear the same mask as her mother. She was alone in the drawing-room now. They had gone upstairs, Mummy loud-voiced, shrill like a fish-wife, common for the first time; and Uncle John pleading, protesting, dragging at her shoulder with ineffectual hands.

'A happy New Year! A happy New Year!'

Hands dragged at her, voices cried in her ear, and the band played loud and gay. It was a triumph, her party; a gala, an overwhelming success. Wherever she looked, faces smiled at her; whenever she listened, she heard her praises sung.

'You're getting more like your mother every day. Isn't it wonderful for you both – just like a couple of sisters!'

Nearly twelve o'clock, and the old year soon would die. Streamers were flung across the restaurant, blue, orange, and green; old men in paper caps threw hot little yellow balls to complete strangers at the next table; coloured paper littered the floor, twined round the feet of the riotous, jostling couples. There was not a square inch of space upon the floor; bodies pressed against each other, hot, perspiring, jigging up and down, leaning against tables, laughing over shoulders. The noise was deafening, the clamour of Babel. Men shouted and whistled, women shrieked hysterically. They looked like a swarm of rats on a sinking ship.

'Happy New Year! Happy New Year!'

'Isn't it marvellous? Aren't you loving it?' someone screamed in her ear.

She tried to respond, she tried to smile back. But she felt every smile was forced and every message insincere.

They knew, these people, they knew about Mummy and Uncle John. They had known for years. Their nods, their smiles, their murmured undertones all proved that they understood. And now they waited for the next step in the game: the first jealous looks, the first signs of rivalry. 'How lovely you've grown!' Laughing behind their hands: 'Of course, they share him.'

They stood in a circle, joining hands, Mummy, she, and Uncle John. 'Should Auld Acquaintance Be Forgot?' – his voice rang loud above the rest; he smiled at Mummy, sleek and smooth, the perfect tabby-cat.

'Happy New Year, darling,' he said. 'Happy New Year.' And then, when the circle broke, he turned to the daughter; he murmured in her ear: 'It's all right. I've calmed her down. She believes our story now. You and I will manage it somehow, Baby. But – listen – we've got to go slow for a bit; damn slow . . .'

Mazie

Mazie lay on her back, afraid to move. Why was it her heart beat so strange nowadays, never quiet, nor steady, but with a queer thump, thump, and little beats that ran in between, and had no right to be there? She was sure, if she moved, it would leap with a sudden jerk right out of her body, and a great black cloud waved close upon her eyes. That's what had happened last month to poor Dolly.

Quite sudden it took her, after the 'flu, and she was dead before you could say 'knife'.

Mazie could remember going to see her when she was laid out. Beautiful she looked, with her pale face and dark hair against the pillow. Mazie had bought her a small bunch of flowers, and put them beside her. Not much, of course, but somehow, it seemed heartless like to leave Dolly without a word. You never knew when it was going to be your turn. Dolly had used those very words time and time again, and then, before she knew where she was, poor thing, she was gone.

In the night, like the light of a candle. Queer.

Thump – there it was again, knocking about in her chest; almost as if her chest was a door, and there was somebody trying to get in. Yes, that was it, knocking and knocking, trying to get in. Well, it wasn't a scrap of use getting into a state, and worrying herself. What had to be had to be. You couldn't stop what was coming to you, and yet, what would happen if she came over really bad, one night when she was alone, when she had nobody? Would she be able to call for help, to make herself heard on the floor below, or would she just go out in the dark – like Dolly? 'Now, if I start getting afraid,' thought Mazie, 'there's an end to it, and everything will be U.P. So just don't let's start thinking.'

She sat up in bed, and began to pull on her stockings. It wasn't any mortal use being tired like this in the mornings. She saw herself in the cracked mirror on the wall. Cripes! what a face! Like a bit of boiled mutton. If she went about like that, she wouldn't find a dustman to look at her, let alone anything else. If she weren't careful, she'd be hanging round, day after day, and returning home with an empty purse. As it was, she got so tired these days that she scarcely knew what she was up to, and that's a fact.

Who and what she picked up last night, she couldn't tell if she was asked. All she could remember was that he was quiet spoken, and had a light moustache. There had been a bit of bother over the price, too, now she came to think, but she hadn't been done in – not she.

What a life! Ah, that was better! She dabbed the rouge on her cheeks and smothered the whole with a great mask of powder. That was more like a face, that was. Carefully she laid the black on her eyes, and smeared her lips a wet sticky crimson.

Oh! hell, she'd have to take in another inch of her costume.

The skirt was hanging round her waist. A safety-pin would have to do for now. But there was no doubt she was getting thinner every day. Someone had cursed her as a bag of bones the other night – dirty swine.

Her fair hair was greasy, straightish. She must put some money aside and have another perm.

When she was dressed, she drew aside the curtains and opened the window.

Why, it was warm, quite warm. The Spring. A child was playing in the street, without her coat. Funny, the way days suddenly changed like that. Yesterday now, cold and snappy, with a miserable spite of a wind that crept down your spine, and little drops of rain from the grey sky, splashing your silk stockings.

But today, warm, jolly, somehow – and the sun was shining into the room opposite, lighting up a big square of carpet.

Mazie leant out of the window, and sniffed the air. Right high up like that made you forget about the dust and smoke, the long day ahead, the longer night – there was only the roofs of houses here, and the blue sky, covered with little flaky clouds.

A sparrow hopped on to the sill, and nearly toppled over with surprise when he saw her. He gave a startled chirp, and fluttered his wings.

She couldn't help laughing, really.

'Cheeky beggar, you don't get nothing from me,' and she searched the floor for a stray crumb.

Mazie walked along Shaftesbury Avenue, looking at the shops. Strewth! what a dream. Scarlet it was, with golden beads all down the middle, and a long piece of stuff touching the ground on the left side. A regular evening gown. Quite the latest, she'd be bound. There was a big spreading flower on the left shoulder too, ever so handsome. No use going in and asking what it cost; that was the worst of these shops that didn't hang the price in the window. You went in, all swagger and show, and had to come out again, pretending you'd be back in the afternoon. The trouble was they got to know you after a bit, if you were always passing by. 'You were in here the other day, weren't you?' they would say, as nasty as anything. Shop girls in black satin, trying to look superior – the sluts.

Look at that two-piece there, in stockinet. Brown scarf to match. Three and a half guineas. Now, that is value, if you *do* like . . . Dressed in that, and her hair waved, she could collar someone big, some gent, in evening dress after the theatre. Easy as pot. She might even get hold of somebody regular. Gawd! what a hope. To be able to take it peaceful, not turn out like this, day after day, wet or fine.

'Hullo, duck, how's life been treating you?' Mazie turned and saw at her elbow a pale shabby girl, so thin that her hips seemed to stare from her clothes, and a small sunken face – large, empty hollows for her eyes.

'Why,' she stammered. 'Why, it's never Norah?'

'Yeh!' said the girl, in a lost voice, in a voice that came from another world. 'It's me, all right, duck, and no mistake about it. Guess I look a bit of a rag, don't I?'

'What happened to you, Norah?'

'What happens to all of us, sooner or later, my pet. Christ! If I knew who the fellow was, I'd wring his bleeding neck. Here, have a peppermint? Sweetens the breath.'

She held out a crumpled paper bag. Mazie stuffed a couple of bull's eyes in her cheek.

'You look pulled down, dear, and that I will say. A dirty shame, I call it. How did you manage then?'

'Oh, I went to a chap Mollie told me of. You know Mollie? It happened to her last winter. She was as right as rain, she said, after a few days – but it takes people different. I tell you, Mazie, I feel awful bad – my legs seem to tremble under me, and I can't breathe proper. Supposing I'm done in for good, that's what I say to myself? Suppose I'm done in for good? What'll happen?' She pawed at Mazie's shoulder.

'Here, shut up, don't take on so,' said Mazie. 'Who ever heard of such a thing. You take it quiet for a week, if you can, and after that you'll be the same as ever. It ain't nothing. It happens every day to girls. You ought to be more careful.'

'Careful? As if it's anything to do with being careful. I've always been careful enough, God knows. Mazie, I can't rest for a week. Where am I to get the money, how am I to live?'

'I don't know, I'm sure.' Mazie began to shuffle away.

'Couldn't you see your way to helping me at all, duckie? This business took everythink I put by.'

'Oh! Give over nagging, Norah. Maybe I can lend you something, but I'm in a hurry now. Stop blubbing, do. People'll start takin' notice of us. Here – take this – and come and see me tomorrow mornin'. You know my place.' Mazie fumbled in her bag, and gave something to Norah. Then she turned and ran down the stairs of the subway beneath Piccadilly Circus.

'I hate people who whine,' she grumbled, to herself. Try as she could, she found it impossible to push Norah out of her thoughts.

She came out of the subway. She walked along the streets, in any direction. It didn't matter.

111

'What did she want to start frightening me for, anyway,' thought Mazie. 'You don't get caught if you're careful – no, you don't.'

Sullenly she glared at the passers-by. Half-unconsciously she pulled her cheap little fur closer to her throat. It seemed colder somehow. Hullo! What was going on here – for the love of Mike. What was all the crowd about? She dug her elbow into the back of a fat woman. 'D'you want the street to yourself?'

Why – it was a wedding. A wedding at St Martin's. Did you ever? What a lark!

She pushed her way to the front of the crowd gathered at the bottom of the steps.

The wide doors were open, but there was a chap at the top there, who wouldn't let you through. She strained her ears to catch the sound of the organ. Yes, there it was, sounding quiet, soft – as if it was afraid to be heard. People were singing. It was getting louder now, and the voices rose with it. Mazie knew this hymn. She had sung it in school as a kid. Strewth! It took you back a bit. Why didn't that chap open the doors wide, she wanted to go right inside the church, and sit in one of those pews at the back.

She'd snatch hold of a hymn-book and sing louder than any of them. She pictured the church, dark and cool, and the pews filled with the guests – the gents in black, and the women dressed like a dream, smart as paint.

She leant forward slightly, and, through the crack of the door, she saw the long aisle, and there were candles somewhere, and flowers – masses of flowers. Seemed as if they filled the air, like scent – rich scent that cost a pound for a tiny bottle. Amen . . . Soft and low. It was beautiful, you know. Made you feel like crying – made you feel, well – queer.

Now there was silence for a moment. Somebody spoke in a high funny voice. Must be the clergyman, giving a blessing, perhaps. Oh! why wasn't she allowed to stand there, quite quiet in a corner. Not so as anyone would notice, but just to hear, just to see.

'Here – who are you pushing – mind out, can't you?' She turned furiously to a man who was prodding her in the back. 'Some people have no manners.'

Now, listen – wait. The organ was striking up the Wedding March. Oh! what a swing there was to it, and the great bells began to peal, breaking out on the air – and the big doors opened wide. 'Here they come – here they come,' shouted the crowd.

'Thank Gawd, the sun's shining for them,' said Mazie, in feverish excitement, to her neighbour. The bride and bridegroom came out upon the steps. They hesitated a second, shy, smiling, dazzled by the light, and then passed quickly down into the cars that waited below.

Just a sudden vision of white, and a veil pushed back from a laughing face – a boy with a white carnation in his button-hole. Bridesmaids in silver, carrying yellow flowers. People shouted, people pressed together – a great cloud of confetti fell upon the bride. Mazie dashed to the edge of the pavement, her eyes shining, her face scarlet. 'Hooray! Hooray!' she shouted, waving her hand.

There were patches of colour on the water, splintered crimson and gold, that danced and twisted beneath Westminster Bridge. The sun was setting, and the orange sky flung golden patterns on to the windows of the Houses of Parliament.

There seemed to be a mist over things. A mist that was part of the pale smoke, curling from the tall chimneys of the factories, and part of the river itself, a white breath rising from the mud banks beneath the swift-flowing tide. Mazie leant against the wall of the Embankment, gazing into the water. She dragged off her hat, and the wind blew her hair behind her ears.

Her feet ached in her tight black shoes, she was tired, dead beat. On the go all day, and doing nothing at that! Just moving about from place to place, you know how it is, when you meant in the morning to spend a quiet day. But what with one thing and another, the wedding, a bite of lunch, a bit of shopping and then, before you knew where you were – evening again.

Oh! but it was nice here by the water, peaceful somehow. Look at that cloud of birds by the bridge there, fat little grey fellows, they didn't go hungry at any rate.

What were they, pigeons? She was blowed if she knew one bird from another.

My! And that boat there, that long barge affair in the middle of the river.

It was a picture, really. She'd like to be on it, sitting by the funny steering thing, and just floating off anywhere – past all the warehouses and the wharves, past the dirty smelly docks, to the sea – the sea. She gave a gasp at the thought. Yes, it was true. At the end, right at the end of this long brown twisting river, the sea waited. No mud there, no filth – no musty old smoke. Just a whole lot of blue water going on for ever – and white waves splashing in your face. It wouldn't matter a scrap where you went – you'd lean your head on the side of the barge, and dangle your hand in the water. No more trudging along pavements, no more blasted waiting about – hanging about. Just rest, your heart beating softly, evenly, and sleep – sleep a long long time.

'I say, you're not going to fall in, are you?' Mazie almost jumped out of her skin.

'Strewth, you didn't give me half a start, did you?' she said angrily, glaring at the young man who had spoken to her. And then, because he smiled in such a kind friendly way, she couldn't help smiling back.

'I was looking at that silly old barge, you know, and there I was thinking to myself how I'd like to be there, swinging along, as happy as you please – no more worries, no more nothink. Guess I'm soft in the head, eh.'

The young man lit a cigarette and leant against the wall beside her.

'I've felt like that, too,' he told her. 'It's strange, isn't it, how it comes over you suddenly, that longing to break right away, to clear out. I've been down by the Docks after midnight, sometimes, when the night is black, and you can't see anything but the dark boiling water, and the lights of the ships at anchor. Then there'll come the long queer wail of a siren out of the darkness, and you'll see a red light move, and you'll hear the churning throb of a propeller – and the faint outline of a big ship passes you – right in the centre of the river – outward bound.'

Something tightened in Mazie's throat.

'Go on,' she whispered.

'That's right,' he said. 'She'll pass you by in the middle of the river, and you'll fancy you hear the clanking of chains on a deck, and the hoarse cries of men. Right down the Channel she goes, past Greenwich and Barking, past the flat green swamp, past Gravesend – into the sea. And you stand on the edge of the dock, just a little black smudge – left behind.'

'That's what we are,' repeated Mazie slowly, 'a crowd of little black smudges – and nobody knows and nobody cares. A funny world, eh?'

'Yes – a queer world.'

They were silent for a moment. Mazie watched the golden patches on the water.

'I wish – oh! I wish I was rich,' she said. 'D'you know what I'd do? I'd take a first class ticket at a station, and I'd get into a train, a train that goes to a place as I've seen on posters.'

'What's it called?'

'I don't know – but if I saw it written down, I'd remember. There's sands there, golden sands, and a wide stretch of sea. There's little boats too, with brown sails – which you hire for a shilling an hour – and there's donkeys with ribbons in their ears – running up and down the sands. D'you know what I'd do if I went there – d'you know? I'd pull my shoes and stockings off, like a kid, and tuck up my skirt, and I'd stand in the water just as long as I liked – and splash with my feet.'

He laughed at her.

'You don't want much, do you?' he said. 'I bet that place you mean is Southend.'

'That's it, you've got it,' she nearly fell over in her excitement. 'That's where I'm going when I'm rich. And I'm going to build a little farm, on a cliff, with cows and chickens, ever so homely.'

She looked across the river, and saw no more factory chimneys, but a small, very white cottage and a neat garden, trimmed with stiff flowers. There'd be a hammock strung between two trees. Oh! Why did the picture make her feel so tired again, why did her head ache once more, and that old sleepless devil of a heart start thumping, thumping in her breast?

Mechanically she drew her puff from her bag, and covered her face with a white cloud. She smeared the lipstick on her mouth.

'Silly – how it is, when you gets thinking,' she said aloud.

The light was gone now. The river passed beneath the bridge, brown and swollen. The barge had vanished. The sky was grey and overcast. And the man had forgotten the ship that passed out of the docks at midnight, outward bound.

He was somebody now who jingles the change in his pockets, who smiles a slow false smile. The man who passes – the man in the street.

He touched Mazie's shoulder.

'Look here, what about it? My place is only just round the corner . . .'

It was evening. They sat in a corner of a restaurant in Soho. The room was thick with smoke, and the smell of rich food. The woman at the table opposite was drunk. Her red hair slopped over her eye, and she kept screaming with laughter. The men filled her glass, digging each other in the ribs, and winking.

'Now then, sweetheart – just another little glass, just a drop – a tiny drop.'

Mazie sat at the table by the window. Her companion was a fat Jew with a yellow face.

His plate was heaped with spaghetti and chopped onion. He was enjoying his meal – a stream of dribble ran from

117

the corner of his mouth and settled on his beard. He looked up from his food, and smiled at Mazie, showing large gold teeth.

'Eat, little love, eat.' He opened his mouth and laughed, smacking his fat wet lips. He bent down and felt her legs under the table. He stared, breathing heavily.

There was a piano and a violin in the restaurant. The violin squeaked and quivered and the piano crashed, and hammered. The sound rose above the voices of the people, drowning their conversation, drumming into their ears. They had to shout to one another.

Mazie forced some curry down her throat. No use thinking about being tired, no use listening to her beating heart.

'Aren't you going to order somethink to drink?' she screamed, above the wail of the violin.

A low droning voice sounded behind her. She looked out of the window.

An old woman stood there, a filthy dirty old hag with bleary eyes and loose slobbery lips. A wisp of grey hair fell over her wrinkled forehead. She held out her hand, and whimpered, 'Give us a copper, dearie, just a copper. I ain't 'ad a bite all day. I'm starvin', dearie. Be kind – there's a love, be kind to a poor old woman who's got no one to look after her.'

'Oh! go away, do,' said Mazie.

'I don't ask for much, dearie, only a copper to get meself a bite of food. There's no one to give me anything now.' The terrible voice whined on and on.

'I was young like you once, dearie, young and 'and-some And gentlemen gave me dinners, too, and paid me well, they did. Not so very long ago, neither, dearie. You'll

118

know what it is one day, when you're old and ugly, you'll stand here then and beg for charity, same as me now. You wait, dearie, you wait.'

'Go away,' said Mazie. 'Go away.'

The woman crept along the street, wrapping her shawl round her, and cursing and muttering to herself. The fat Jew heaved himself up in his chair, and poured the wine into Mazie's glass.

'Drink, little love,' he pleaded. But Mazie did not hear.

She was thinking of Norah in Shaftesbury Avenue, with her pinched white face and her words – 'Sooner or later.'

She thought of the busy streets packed with people, jostling her, shoving her from side to side. She remembered the wedding, and the smell of flowers – the smiling girl who stepped into the waiting car.

She saw the golden patches on the river as the sun set, and a barge that floated away to the open sea – and a man's voice whispering in her ear, a man's hand touching her shoulder.

She heard the old woman whining. 'You'll know what it is one day, dearie,' and then creeping away to huddle for the night in the shelter of a theatre wall, her head in her lap. Two drops of rain fell on to the pavement.

Mazie seized her glass of wine and drank.

A shudder ran through her. The music wailed, the light blazed, the Jew smiled.

'Here,' shouted Mazie, 'why don't they play somethink gay? Waiter! Tell them to play somethink lively, somethink gay . . .'

Nothing Hurts for Long

She had the window flung open as she dressed. The morning was cold, but she liked to feel the sharp air on her face, stinging her, running like little waves over her body; and she slapped herself, the colour coming into her skin, the nerves tingling. She sang, too, as she dressed. She sang when she took her bath, her voice seeming rich and powerful as the water fell and the steam rose, and later, before the open window, she bent and swayed, touching her toes with her fingers, stretching her arms above her head.

She permitted herself the luxury of fresh linen. Conscious of extravagance, she drew the neat pleated little pile, straight from the laundry, out of the drawer beneath her dressing-table.

Her green dress was back from the cleaner's. It looked as good as new and the length was quite right, although she had worn it last winter as well. She cut the disfiguring tabs from the collar, and sprayed the dress with scent to take away the smell of the cleaner's.

She felt new all over. From her head to her shoes, and the body beneath her clothes was warm and happy. Her hair had been washed and set the day before, brushed behind her ears without a parting, like the actress she admired.

She could imagine his face as he stared at her, his funny

smile that ran from one ear to the corner of his mouth, and his eyebrow cocked, then his eyes half-closing, and holding out his arms – 'Darling, you look marvellous – marvellous.' When she thought about it she felt a queer pain in her heart because it was too much . . . She stood before the window a moment, smiling, breathing deeply, and then she ran down the stairs singing at the top of her voice, the sound of her song taken up by the canary in his cage in the drawing-room. She whistled to him, laughing, giving him his morning lump of sugar, and he hopped from side to side on his perch, his eyes beady, his tiny head fluffy and absurd after his bath. 'My sweet,' she said, 'my sweet,' and pulled the curtain so that the sun could get to him.

She glanced round the room, smiling, her finger on her lip. She pummelled at an imaginary crease in a cushion, she straightened the picture over the mantelpiece, she flicked a minute particle of dust from the top of the piano. His eyes, in the photograph on her desk, followed her round the room, and she paraded before it self-consciously, as though he were really there, patting a strand of her hair, glancing in the mirror, humming a tune. 'I must remember to fill the room with flowers, of course,' she thought, and immediately she saw the flowers she would buy, daffodils or hard mauve tulips, and where they would stand.

The telephone rang from the dining-room. It was really the same room, divided by a curtain, but she called it the dining-room. 'Hullo – Yes, it's me speaking. No, my dear. I'm afraid I couldn't possibly. Yes. Yes, he comes back today. I expect him about seven. Oh! but you don't understand, there are tons of things to see to. I like to think I have the whole day. No, I'm not silly, Edna. Wait until you're married, then you'll see. Yes, rather, we'll go to a film next week – I'll let you know. Good-bye.'

She put down the receiver, and shrugged her shoulders. Really – how ridiculous people were. As if she could possibly go out or do anything when he was coming home at seven. Why, for the past fortnight now she had remembered to book nothing for Tuesday. Although he would not be back until the evening it did not make any difference. It was his day.

She crossed the absurd space known as the hall and went into the kitchen. She tried to look important, the mistress of the house, ready to give her orders, but her smile betrayed her and the dimple at the corner of her mouth.

She sat on the kitchen table, swinging her legs, and Mrs Cuff stood before her with a slate. 'I've been thinking, Mrs Cuff,' she began, 'that he always does so enjoy saddle of mutton. What do you say?'

'Yes – he is fond of his mutton, ma'am.'

'Would it be terribly extravagant? Do saddles cost a lot?'

'Well, we've been very careful, this week, haven't we?'

'Yes – Mrs Cuff, that's what I thought. And for lunch I can have a boiled egg and some of that tinned fruit, it'll be heaps. But this evening, if you think you could cope with a saddle – and p'raps – what does one eat with it? – Oh! mashed potatoes, done his favourite way – and Brussels sprouts, and jelly.'

'Yes, ma'am, that would be nice.'

'And – Mrs Cuff – could we possibly have that kind of roly-pudding he likes with jam inside? You know – one is terribly surprised to see the jam.'

'Just as you wish, ma'am.'

'I expect he'll be frightfully hungry, don't you? I'm sure it's horrid in Berlin. I think that's all, don't you? It doesn't seem only three months, does it, it seems three years since he's been gone?'

'Oh! It has been dull, ma'am. It will be a different place with him back.'

'He's always so gay, isn't he, Mrs Cuff? Never dreary and depressed like other people.'

'Please, ma'am, while I remember it — we want some more Ronuk.'

'I don't think I've ever seen him in a bad temper. What did you say, Mrs Cuff? Ronuk? Is it stuff for swilling round basins?'

'No, ma'am — for cleaning the floors.'

'I'll try and remember. All right then, an egg for my lunch and the saddle to-night.' She went upstairs to see that his dressing-room was tidy.

'Some day I'll find you—
Moonlight behind you,'

she sang, and opened the cupboards in case the suits he had left behind, and might want to wear to-morrow, had not been brushed. The shabby old leather coat, not good enough for Berlin, still hung on its peg. She fingered the sleeve, and pressed her nose against the motoring cap that smelt of the stuff he put on his hair.

The photograph of herself swung crookedly from a drawing-pin on the wall, curling at the corners. She pretended not to notice it, hurt that he had never bothered to get a frame, never taken it to Berlin. 'I suppose men think in a different way to women,' she said to herself, and suddenly she closed her eyes and stood quite still without moving, because it had come to her swiftly like a wave covering her from head to foot, a wave of the sea and the sun, exquisite and strange, the realisation that in less than ten hours he really would be next to her – they would be together again – and they loved each other, and it was all true.

She had filled the two rooms with flowers, and had even drawn the curtains separating the dining-room aside, so that the space should be magnified. The canary still sang in his cage. 'Louder, sweet, louder,' she called and it seemed that the house was filled with his singing – a high, joyous clamour straight from his small bursting heart – and it mingled in some indescribable fashion with the beam of gold dust shining upon the carpet, the last lingering pattern made by the setting sun.

She poked the fire and dusted the ashes in the grate, thinking as she did so how, in the evening, she would be doing the same thing, and would remember this moment. The curtains would be drawn then, and the lamps lit, and the bird quiet in his cage, and he lounging in the arm-chair by the fire, stretching out his legs, watching her lazily. 'Stop fussing – and come here,' while she turned towards him, smiling, her hand on his knee. And she would think – 'This afternoon I was alone and now I'm looking back remembering it,' and the thought would be somehow delicious like a secret vice. She hugged her knees, and stared at the fire, childishly excited at the memory of the large, expensive bottle of bath salts she had bought that morning and put on his dressing-table, as well as the bowl of flowers.

When the telephone rang she sighed regretfully, unwilling to leave the fire, alter her position and be taken from the queer, lonely pleasure of her dreams to the conversation of someone who did not matter, forced and unreal.

'Hullo,' she said, and there came from the other end of the wire a little choking sound, the pitiful drawn breath of one who is crying, who cannot control her tears.

'Is that you? It's May . . . I had to ring you. I – I'm so desperately unhappy,' and the voice trailed off, choked, suffocated.

'Why,' she said, 'what on earth is the matter? Tell me, quick, can I do anything? Are you ill?'

She waited a moment, and then the voice came again, muffled and strange.

'It's Fred. It's all over – we've finished. He wants me to divorce him – he's stopped loving me.' Then she heard a quiver and a sharp intake of breath, and the sound of sobbing, hideous, degrading, uncontrolled.

'My poor darling!' she began, amazed and horrified; 'but how perfectly frightful. I can't believe it – Fred – but it's absurd.'

'Please – please – come round and see me,' begged the voice. 'I think I'm going out of my mind – I don't know what I'm doing.'

'Yes – of course. I'll come right away.'

As she put on her things she brushed from her mind the selfish regret she felt at leaving the fire and the book she was reading, and the idea of making toast for tea, all the things that were part of the loveliness of waiting for him, and she gave her thoughts to May, broken and distressed, crying helplessly, her happiness gone from her.

She went in a taxi, because, after all, May was her greatest friend, and one and six was not so much; and that reminded her she had forgotten about the Ronuk. Oh, well! never mind . . . and Mrs Cuff seemed pleased with the saddle of mutton . . . Was he crossing now? She wondered; how awful if he was sick, poor angel, how sweet . . . she must remember to think about May, though; Life was frightful, of course . . . and here she was at the door, thank goodness, only a shilling; still, she would go home in a bus, anyway . . .

May was lying face downwards on a sofa, her head buried in a cushion.

She knelt by her side, patting her shoulder, murmuring senseless little words of comfort.

'May, darling May – you mustn't cry like that, it's so weakening for you; it will pull you down – try not to, please, try and pull yourself together, darling.'

And May lifted her head and showed her face, swollen, disfigured and blotched, so ravaged with her tears that it was shocking, something that should not be seen.

'I can't stop,' May whispered; 'you can't understand what it is – it's tearing at me like a knife, and I can't forget his face as he told me, so cold and different . . . it wasn't him at all, it was somebody else.'

'But it's simply unbelievable, May! Why should Fred suddenly take it into his head to tell you he doesn't love you? He must have been drunk – it can't be true.'

'It is true.' May was tearing her handkerchief to little shreds and biting the ends.

'And it's not sudden, that's the whole thing; it's been coming on for some while. I've never told you – I've never breathed a word to anyone. I kept hoping and praying it was only my imagination, but all the time I knew deep down that everything was wrong.'

'Oh! my poor May. To think I didn't know . . .'

'Don't you understand that there are some things one can't tell, that are too intimate; that I was terrified to breathe, hoping if I kept silent they wouldn't come true?'

'Yes – yes – I see.'

'And then to-day, when there was no longer any doubt, I suppose the agony and terror I had been holding inside could not stay silent any more; I had to give way.'

'Oh! May – darling, darling May!' she said, looking round the room hopelessly, as though by getting up and moving a piece of furniture she could do some good.

'What a beast – what a brute!' she said.

'Oh, he's not that!' said May, staring before her, her voice weary from crying. 'Fred's only a man like other men. They're all the same; they can't help it. I don't blame him. I'm only angry with myself for being such a fool to care.'

'How long have you known?'

'Ever since he came back from America.'

'But, May, darling, that's eight months ago. You surely have not been suffering all this time, keeping it for yourself? It's impossible!'

'Oh, my dear – it hasn't been eight months to me, but an eternity! I don't know if you can realise for one minute the hell that it's been. Never quite being certain, the awful bewildering doubt and pretending that nothing was wrong. Then the degradation of trying to please him, of not noticing his manner, of making myself a sort of slave in the hope that he might come back to me. Eight months of misery and shame . . .'

'Oh, if only I could have helped!' she began; and she was thinking, 'But these things don't happen to people – they can't; it's only in plays.'

'Help isn't any use,' said May; 'you have to go through it alone. I believe every moment has made its mark upon me, hurting and branding my heart – every moment from the very first until the last.'

'But, May, darling, why should America have made any difference?'

'Because going away does make a difference to men. Don't you see that when Fred wasn't with me he forgot about wanting to be with me, and once he forgot that he was ready to forget anything. And a different way of living, and seeing new things, and meeting new people.'

'But still . . .'

'Directly he came back I knew what had happened. I can't describe to you the difference there was. Nothing marked or striking. But a queer, subtle change. Little things he said, his manner, even his voice – he talked louder, like someone who is trying to bluff a secret – can you understand? The very first day he was home I saw – and I pushed it aside but it hurt – and it went on hurting until to-day – and now I know at last what I've tried to hide.'

'Is he in love with somebody else?' she whispered.

'Yes . . .' and the voice broke again, the tears welling up into her eyes, 'yes . . . there is some woman, of course – behind it; but it's not only that – it's our life he doesn't want any more, this house – me – everything. He wants to break away altogether. He doesn't want ties, or a home – he talks of going back to America . . .'

'But Fred to behave like that – and all this time when

I've seen you together, not a sign from either of you – my poor May!'

And though her words were full of pity and she held May close to her, trying to comfort her, she was aware that her heart could not hold any real sympathy, and that the sight of May's tears awoke even a sense of irritation and contempt which was difficult to banish, and she said to herself, with her eye on the clock, 'I suppose I can't feel this because I know it couldn't ever happen to me.'

'I haven't thought yet how I'm going to live,' said May; 'all I know is that it's impossible to suffer more than I have suffered already. Those terrible months – and then to-day.'

'Don't cry, darling,' she said, and she was thinking, 'Oh, dear! is she going to begin all over again? It's really too much. Besides, it's getting late.'

'Don't you think,' she said gently, 'that a large brandy and soda would do you good? And your poor head must be splitting. If you go upstairs and go to bed with a nice hot bottle – and two aspirins – and try to forget . . .'

May smiled at her through her tears.

'If you think that is a cure,' she said. 'No – I'm all right . . . don't worry about me. You must get back, too . . . he's coming home to-night, isn't he? I've only just remembered.'

'Yes,' she said indifferently, trying not to parade her pleasure, and to make up for it she seized hold of May's hands and said, 'Darling – if you knew how terribly I feel for you, if only I could share it. What a wicked shameful thing life is – God shouldn't let it happen – this horrid, miserable world, why were we ever born . . .' and the tears came into her eyes, too, and they rocked together on the sofa, and she was thinking, her heart fluttering with absurd

130

joy and the thought of his face before her – 'Oh, dear – I'm so happy!'

Finally she tore herself away, the hands of the clock pointing to half-past six. 'Of course I'll come to-morrow,' and supposing his train is early, she thought, and she wondered how she could possibly keep from smiling before poor May. 'Darling, are you sure you are all right left alone?' she said; and not waiting for the answer she was dragging on her coat and her hat, looking for her bag, trembling with the excitement which it was impossible to control any longer.

'Good-night, darling,' she said, kissing her fondly, patting the blotched, disfigured face which roused in her an insane desire to laugh ('How vile of me,' she thought), and she searched feverishly for some parting, consoling phrase; and because in half an hour she would be with him, blotted against him, losing herself, caring for no one, drunk and absurd – she said happily, her face radiant as she stood on the doorstep, 'It's all right; nothing hurts for long.'

For the fourth time she made up the fire, stabbing at the coal with the tongs, sparks flying on to the carpet, and she did not notice. She jumped up from her chair and touched the flowers, she sat down to the piano and played the bar of a tune, only to run across to the window and pull aside the curtain, thinking she heard a taxi.

She was not sure how she wanted him to find her. Crouched by the fire perhaps, or lying in a chair, or putting on the gramophone. The clock in the dining-room struck eight. 'Oh! but it must be fast,' she thought wildly, and called to the kitchen, 'Mrs Cuff, what is the right time?'

'Past eight, ma'am, and the dinner is spoiling.'

'Can't you keep it hot?'

131

'I can keep it hot, ma'am, but the joint is overdone and the vegetables are cooked. Such a pity. He's not going to enjoy it much.'

'I can't understand why he is late, Mrs Cuff. I've rung through to the station, and the train came in punctually at six forty-five. What can have happened?'

She walked from the dining-room to the kitchen, biting her nails, wondering if she was going to be sick. Surely he would have let her know if he had been coming by a later train. 'He'll be so ravenous when he does arrive he'll eat anything – if it's burnt to cinders,' she said. She was not hungry herself; it would have choked her to touch the dinner.

'He's always up in the clouds,' she thought; 'he probably does not realise the time. That's the worst of being temperamental. All the same . . .'

She put on a gramophone record, but the noise grated; the voice of Maurice Chevalier sounded high-pitched and ridiculous.

She went and stood before the looking-glass. Perhaps he would creep in suddenly and stand behind her, and put his hands on her shoulders, and lean his face against hers.

She closed her eyes. Darling! Was that a taxi? No – Nothing.

'This wasn't how I imagined it at all,' she thought. She threw herself in a chair and tried to read. Hopeless – what nonsense people wrote, anyway. Why was one supposed to take an interest in the life of someone who did not exist? She wandered over to the piano once more and began to strum.

'Some day I'll find you,
Moonlight behind you,'

she sang, but her fingers were heavy and her voice a poor thin whisper of a thing that went flat and could not strike the right note. The canary in the cage pricked up his ears. He started his song, and soon it filled the room, deafening her, shrill and absurd, so loud that she flung the cover on to his cage in irritation.

'Be quiet, can't you, you horrid little thing!' she said. It was being so different from the morning, and as she poked the fire again she remembered that moment during the afternoon when she had smiled to herself and thought, 'I shall remember this minute.'

And the chair was still empty, and the room looked lifeless and dull, and she was a little girl whose mouth turned down at the corners, who bit the ends of her hair, who wriggled with hunched shoulders, sniffing in a hankie, 'It isn't fair.'

Soon she had to go upstairs again to do her face, because she had dressed herself all ready for him at half-past nine. Her face wanted doing again. Her nose must be powdered, her lips lightly touched (the stuff did come off so), and her hair brushed away from her face in the new way.

As she took a final peep in the glass she thought how cheap she was making herself – any girl waiting for a man – squalid, like birds who paraded before each other, and it seemed to her that the face that stared at her from the mirror, pretty and smiling, was not the real her at all, was forced and insincere; the real her was a frightened girl who did not care how she looked, whose heart was beating, who wanted only to run out into the street and beg him to come home to her . . .

Then she stood quite still – because surely that was a taxi drawing up to the front door, and surely that was the sound of a key in the lock, and weren't those voices in the hall, suitcases dumped down, and Mrs Cuff coming out of the kitchen, and his voice? For a moment she did not move; it was as though something rose in her throat, stifling her, and something crept down into her legs, paralysing her – and she wanted to go quickly and hide, locking herself somewhere. Then the wave of excitement broke over her once more, and she ran out of the bedroom and stood at the head of the staircase, looking down at him in the hall below.

He was bending over his suitcase, doing something with his keys. 'You might take these things up right away, Mrs Cuff,' he was saying; and then he straightened himself, hearing her step on the stair above, and he looked up and said, 'Hullo, darling.'

How funny – why, he had got fatter surely, or was it just his coat? And he must have cut himself shaving, because he had a silly little bit of plaster on his chin.

She went down the stairs slowly, trying to smile, but odd somehow, shy.

'I've been so worried,' she said, 'what ever happened? You must be absolutely famished.'

'Oh! I missed my connection,' he said, 'I thought you would guess. It's all right, Mrs Cuff, I had my dinner on the train.'

Had his dinner? But that was not how she had planned it.

He kissed her hurriedly, patting her shoulder as though she were a little girl, and then he laughed, and said, 'Why – what on earth have you done to your hair?'

She laughed too, pretending she did not mind. 'I've had it washed – it's nothing, just a bit untidy.' They went into the drawing-room.

'Come and get warm,' she said.

But he did not sit down, he lounged about, jingling the money in his pockets.

'Of course I would come back and find a lousy fog,' he said. 'God – what a country.'

'Is it foggy?' she said. 'I'd not noticed it.' And then there was a pause for a moment, and she looked at him – Yes, he was fatter, different somehow – and she said stupidly 'How did you like Berlin?'

'Oh! it's a grand place,' he said, 'London can't compare with it. The atmosphere, the life there, the people, everything. They know how to live.' And he smiled, rocking on his heels, remembering it; and she thought how terrible it was that he was seeing things in his mind now that she would never see, going over things he had done that she would never know.

'Fancy,' she said, and she knew she hated Berlin, and the people, and the life. She did not want to hear about it – and yet supposing he did not tell her, but kept it to himself, wouldn't that be worse? 'Oh!' he said suddenly, striking his forehead, a stupid theatrical gesture – not impulsive but planned. 'By Jove – I must telephone. I'd quite forgotten. Some people who are over here from Berlin.'

'Telephone?' she said, her heart sick, 'but, darling, you've only just come back.'

'I promised though, rather important,' he said, and kissed her as though he were saying 'There now – be a good girl,' and already he had pushed aside the curtains, and was lifting the receiver, and giving the number. It tripped off his tongue, she thought, he did not have to look it up in the book.

She went and crouched by the fire, cold for no reason,

and tired. She felt empty inside – perhaps it was because she hadn't had any dinner.

He had got on to his friends. He was talking German – and she did not understand. A flow of hideous stupid words, and he kept laughing – surely these friends couldn't be as funny as all that? Why was he laughing? She thought he would never finish. And then he came back through the curtains, red in the face, smiling.

'Well,' he said, talking rather loudly, 'tell me all the news.' Perhaps he felt that after all it was her turn. She felt herself closing up, shy, stupid. She remembered. May and her husband. No – she could not tell him about that, it was as if – as if it wasn't the right moment, it was too soon – besides.

'Oh! I can't think,' she said. 'There doesn't seem to be anything to tell.' He laughed, and his laugh turned into a yawn. 'How's the old bird?' he said, glancing carelessly at the cage, not really wanting to know.

'He's all right,' she said.

He sprawled in a chair, still yawning, his mouth wide open, and she knew as she looked at him that it was not just her fancy, it was not just imagination, but, besides being fatter, he was different in another way – altered, queer – *changed*.

He whistled softly, his eyes staring into space. Then he said slowly, 'Gosh – time's a funny thing. To think that at this moment last night I was in Berlin.'

She smiled nervously, anxious to please, but something stabbed her heart like a sharp little knife, twisting and turning – and into her mind ran the words over and over again: 'It's all right, nothing hurts for long – nothing hurts for long.'

Week–End

When they motored down to the country on Friday evening they scarcely spoke to one another at all. They both of them felt that words would spoil the perfect harmony. He sat at the steering-wheel, intent on his driving and the straight road before him, one hand directing the car and the other around her shoulders. She leant against him, her hands in her lap, and every now and again she sighed and murmured inarticulate sounds of appreciation.

He seemed to understand those sounds, because he answered them in his own way, smiling from time to time, his knee just touching hers.

Their minds were blank and foolish, empty of consecutive thought. Sometimes she glanced at him sideways, and it came to her presently that she adored the way his hair grew at the back of his neck. She did not notice the funny patches of sun-burn on his forehead that reddened with every mile. He caught a glimpse of a dark curl under a beret that twisted upwards in the right way, yet missed the smear of powder that ran patchily on her nose. They were in love.

'You see,' he told her once, 'the marvellous thing about us is that we are such companions. I felt that about you from the first. No effort, no straining after effect. I can be perfectly natural with you. When I think of all the other women one has known—' and he broke off, laughing, shrugging his shoulders. After all, it would not hurt her to believe that there had been other women.

'Yes,' she had said: 'that's what I feel, too. At last I can be myself – there's no need to pretend any more. I can relax and be at peace.' As she said this, she made her voice sound sad, a little tired, hoping by the inflexion she might suggest that hitherto, her life had been too strong, too vital – that she was one of those who had burnt the candle at both ends.

'Peace,' he said slowly. 'Yes; how I longed for peace out in India. You haven't any conception, my darling, what life does to one out there.' He had lived very comfortably in Madras for six years, but there was no need to go into all that. She had such romantic ideas of India; she might imagine him pig-sticking, in white breeches; studying Yoga, perhaps.

'I can picture you,' she told him, 'working and riding under that fierce sun, while I drifted aimlessly in London, leading my useless, butterfly life – going from party to party.' She laughed, bitterly, she hoped, thinking she was conjuring in his mind the vision of night-club after night-club, nigger bands, bored sophistication – anything but the slightly formal evenings in Kensington to which she had been accustomed.

'It's wonderful, isn't it,' he said, 'how we understand each other. We love the same things; we think alike; we disagree over nothing. I mean, it's absolutely terrific the – well – I tell you—' He broke off lamely; words could not express his feelings.

'Darling!' she said.

When they arrived, the moon was shining on the water,

and the tide was high. The waves broke gently on the beach below the house. 'I've often dreamed about places like this,' she said vaguely, spreading out her arms. She never dreamt; but no matter. 'I've imagined lying on hot, white sand, with a cloudless sky above, and next to me someone I could love, who would understand. Someone who would give me peace.'

'My sweet!' he murmured. She rather harped on peace, he thought. He was wondering whether it would be possible to hire a speed-boat for her, with some reliable boatman in charge. 'We'll get a boat tomorrow, shall we?' he said. 'And sail away from all this to the horizon.' His voice was dramatic, he turned his profile to the sky. Swiftly she changed her mood to tune with his.

'You and I together, sailing towards the stars,' she said. They felt so romantic, so adventurous, like Vikings almost.

By midday on Saturday they had little names for one another, and they talked in a special language. It was impossible for either of them to make a statement without lisping and pouting, without stamping their feet and clapping their hands. They had passed from a fatuous self-content to a strange senility.

'Mousie wants to go bathe,' she said; and she was tall and dark, and she would not see thirty again. 'Hoosie wants go bathe, too,' he said. And they splashed each other and played ring-o'-roses in the sea.

'Hoosie's so big and strong,' she told him, as they lay on their backs in the sun; 'that's why Mousie loves Hoosie so much.' She ran her fingers up and down his arm. He shivered slightly; bathing did not agree with him.

'What's for lunch?' he said, slapping his white, dead fingers. 'I don't know about you, but I'm hungry.'

She felt hurt, suddenly, a little rebuffed. 'I'll go and see,' she said. He repented, though; he saw the shadow between them. 'Hoosie kiss Mousie first,' he said.

She smiled, and the cloud passed away from the sun. 'We do love each other, don't we?' she said.

'Yes, darling.'

She stumbled up the beach to the house, trailing her wet wrapper behind her. For the first time he noticed the calves of her legs were big without stockings.

They rested after lunch until five o'clock. The sky was still clear, and the sea without a tremor. 'Is Hoosie going to take Mousie in a boat?' she asked.

He remembered his promise with misgiving. What a bore. Was she going to drag him out? 'Hoosie will do anything Mousie wants,' he said, yawning.

They walked down to the little quay to inspect the boats.

'Let's have that lovely red one, darling, it will just match my beret,' she suggested.

'Mousie wants red boatie,' he said absently, but he was wondering whether he could manage the engine.

'Quite simple, sir,' the fellow explained. 'Foolproof. A child could run her. Here's your spark; here's your throttle – adjust your lever, so – half-open. Give her three swings, then open up.'

'What?' he said. 'What? I don't follow. Say it again.' He glanced over his shoulder to see if she had heard. She was settling herself among the cushions; she was not looking. The fellow started the engine in one swing, and in a moment they were away, the boatman waving encouragement from the quay. He gripped the tiller, glancing anxiously to right and left.

'Clever Hoosie, to manage boatie so well,' she told him.

He swallowed, and stuck out his jaw. They were heading for the open sea. Thank God the water was smooth. He began to feel more at his ease; the light wind ruffled his hair, the spray danced in his face.

'Darling, you look so wonderful!' she screamed.

He smiled. Sweet little Mousie. He steered the boat towards a sheltered bay.

'What's the time?' she asked sleepily. He woke with a start. How long had they been anchored in there? He could not remember. The sun had gone from the bay; the water looked grey and cold. They both shivered, and she reached for her coat. 'Mousie wants to go home,' she said.

He tried to remember what the fellow had told him about starting the engine. Open the thing how much? – pull which lever? He went on swinging without success, barking his knuckles every time. 'Damn, blast and hell!' he swore, sucking his fingers, the skin rubbed raw.

'Naughty Hoosie!' she scolded.

'Well, try the blithering thing yourself,' he said.

'I don't pretend to know anything about boats,' he said, exhausted. 'The beastly engine is a dud; it won't work. Good God! These fellows ought to be shot for hiring out a boat like this. Look here—' A screw came away in his hands.

'You pulled it off yourself; I saw you,' she said. 'I don't believe you know how it does go.'

'That's right, blame me,' he said. 'Whose idea was it, anyway, yours or mine? I was perfectly content as we were. I didn't want to hire the blasted boat.'

'Well, my dear, if I'd known you were so incapable, do you think I'd have come out in it?' she said. 'Look at your face – all covered in oil smears. If you knew what you looked like—'

How like a woman, he thought, cursing him, when he had tried to please her. 'Well, we're in a fine mess,' he said gloomily. 'I don't know what to do.' He shivered; he put on a mackintosh. She was suddenly aware of the patch of sunburn on his forehead. His hair was thin on the top, too. She felt irritable, cold, and bored.

'Can't you shout or wave?' she said. 'Surely someone will hear?'

The beach and the cliffs were deserted, though; there was not a soul in sight. His 'Cooee' sounded so ridiculous, she thought, shrill and hateful, like a Boy Scout's. The call got on her nerves. 'Oh, do stop!' she said. 'It's obviously no good.'

He began blowing on his hands. 'I hope the sea won't get up,' he said. 'I'm a rotten sailor. The slightest motion makes me sick.'

She stared at him frozenly. 'I thought you were good at these sort of things,' she said. He flushed irritably. 'D'you think I'm an explorer, or what?' he said. 'I don't mind telling you that exposure is very bad for me; I get chills very easily. A few hours of this is enough to lay me off for weeks.'

'Well, surely you've been used to roughing it in India?' she said, with a shrug of her shoulders.

'My dear girl, do you think India is a sort of movie land for film stars? Don't show your ignorance. I had a very comfortable house in Madras, with ten servants to look after me.'

'Pity some of them aren't here now,' she said icily.

They were silent for some minutes. The tide had turned and was coming in fast, rocking the boat from side to side.

142

'Look here,' he said, 'I don't like this at all. We're probably in very great danger. I don't like it.'

'You might have thought of that before you brought me out here,' she snapped. 'All you cared about was showing off in that idiotic way. What on earth did you anchor in this horrible bay for anyway?'

'Oh, it's my fault that we anchored, is it? Didn't you ask me to make love to you?' he said.

'Ask you! I like that! Do you think it gives me any pleasure to be messed about in this dirty, uncomfortable boat?' she said.

'Well, by heaven, I certainly wouldn't have done so if you hadn't chucked yourself at me,' he said.

'Oh, so you accuse me of making myself cheap, do you?' she said. 'I suppose you'll be saying next that it was I who suggested coming down here for the week-end?'

'My poor child, it was pretty obvious that you wanted to, wasn't it?'

'I don't know if you realise that you are talking like a cad and a liar. Nobody has ever said things like this to me before.'

'They probably never had the chance,' he said.

'You're appallingly conceited, aren't you?' she said. 'And I suppose you think this is the first week-end I've ever spent with anyone in my life?'

'I can't say you give me the impression of having vast fields of experience,' he said.

'Thank you,' she said. 'And you may as well know that it was my first week-end, and I don't mind telling you now that it's been the biggest disappointment of my life, from every point of view.'

It began to rain, a few spots at first, then a drizzle, finally settling to a steady downpour for the evening. The sky darkened, and the boat rocked on the rising tide. He leant against the gunwale, a thin, pitiful figure in his damp bathing suit and mackintosh, his nose blue with the cold.

She suddenly remembered a picture book of her childhood and an illustration of a little goblin called the Inky Imp. What an absurd object he was! How inefficient; how lacking in courage. She blew her nose, she began to cough. He turned away, so that he could not see her blotched and streaky face, the wet rat's tail of hair that drooped upon her shoulders. She looked sulky, peaked, incredibly unattractive. She reminded him of a bedraggled mouse. Mouse. The name suited her, by thunder!

'Thank the Lord we don't have to go on talking that perishing language, anyway,' he thought.

She watched him sullenly for a while, then stubbed him with her foot. 'If you're going to be sick, for God's sake be sick,' she said, 'and have done with it.'

They were towed back to the harbour by a fishing boat, at five in the morning. Already he was suffering agonies with rheumatism in his feet, and he had a chill on the liver. She was starting a cold in the head and her right cheek was swollen with neuralgia. They went straight to bed, and slept until the afternoon. They woke to a grey cheerless Sunday, with the rain still pattering against the windows.

They sat in the sitting-room on two hard chairs, while the fire smoked, and they had not even the Sunday papers. Their minds were blank and foolish, empty of consecutive thought. Sometimes she glanced at him and noticed the patch of sunburn on his forehead. He caught a glimpse of the smear of powder on her nose. They were no longer in love.

144

'You see,' he told her, 'the thing is, we aren't companions, really, at all; we don't even like the same things or have one thought in common. It's so hopeless that – well – I tell you—' he broke off lamely, shrugging his shoulders.

'That's what I feel, too,' she said. 'We simply rub each other the wrong way the entire time. You make me restless and miserable.'

'I wish to heaven I was back in India,' he told her.

'I can imagine you,' she laughed bitterly, 'sitting on a stupid office-stool, biting the end of your pen, while I'm being useful canvassing for Members of Parliament at by-elections.'

They listened to the rain and the surf on the shore.

'This is a hateful place,' she said; 'gloomy and depressing; nothing but stretches of heavy sand-dunes. Like a convict settlement.'

'Fool!' he thought, but he was wondering whether it would be possible to hire a car to take them back to town. He was too tired to drive himself.

'It gives me neuralgia just to sit in this appalling room,' she said. But he had not heard. 'Let's get a car,' he said, 'and leave the beastly spot, and go back to London.' His voice was irritable; he peered moodily out of the window, and the rheumatism pricked at his shoulders.

'You and I, driving that way alone?' she said. They were so bored with one another, so tired. A tiny patch of blue appeared in the sky and a blackbird whistled from a tree. They did not see, they did not hear. 'God! it might be the end of the world here,' he said.

When they motored up to London on Sunday evening they scarcely spoke to one another at all.

The Happy Valley

When she first used to see the valley it was in dreams, little odd snatches remembered on waking, and then becoming easily dimmed and lost in the turmoil of the day. She would find herself walking down a path, flanked on either side by tall beech trees, and then the path would narrow to a scrappy muddy footway, tangled and over-grown, with only shrubs about her – rhododendron, azalea, and hydrangea, stretching tentacles across the pathway to imprison her. And then, at the bottom of the valley, there was a clearing in the under-growth, a carpet of moss and a lazy-running stream. The house, too, would come within her line of vision. A wide window on the ground floor, with a rose creeper climbing to the sill, and she herself standing outside this on a terrace of crazy paving. There was so great a sense of peace in her familiarity with the valley and the house that the dream became one she welcomed and expected; she would wander about the forsaken terrace and lean her cheek against the smooth white surface of the house as though it were part of her life, bound up in her, possessed. It was above all things a place of safety, nothing could harm her here. The dream was a thing precious and beloved, that in its own peculiar individual fashion never unfolded itself, nor told a story, nor followed a sequence. Nor did she remember when the dream had come to her for the first time, but it seemed to have grown with her since her illness, almost as if a stray particle of anaesthetic clung to her sleeping mind like a gentle mist.

During the day the dream would go from her, and weeks or months might pass before it came to her again, and then suddenly in the silent hush of morning when the world is asleep and before the first bird stretches his wings, she would be standing on the terrace before the house in the full warmth of the sun, her face turned to the open window. Her dreaming mind, lost to the world and intensely alive in its own dream planet, would quieten and relax, would murmur in solitude, 'I'm here, I'm happy, I'm home again.'

No more than this and no conclusion; it was a momentary state beyond heaven and earth, suspended in time between two strokes of a clock, and so would be vanished again, and she waking to the familiarity of her own bedroom and the beginning of another day. The clatter of breakfast cups, the street noises, the hum of the sweeper on the back stairs, all the usual homely sounds would bring her back to reality with a shudder and a frustrated sense of loss. Since her illness she had become more than ever absent-minded, so her aunt told her; it was like living with a ghost, with someone who was not there. 'Look up, listen, what are you thinking about?' And she would lift her head with a jerk, startled by the demands made upon her. 'Sorry, I wasn't thinking.'

'You're mooning, always mooning,' came the reply, and she would flush sensitively, easily hurt, but wishing for her aunt's sake she could be brilliant and entertaining. She would pucker her forehead in a frown, and steal up to the old school-room and lean her arms on the window-sill, looking down upon the roofs of houses, glad to be alone yet aware of her loneliness, knowing in a strange unconscious fashion that this was a passage of time; she did not belong here, she was waiting for something that would bring her security and peace like the sunken tangled path in her dream, and the house, and the happy valley.

The first thing he said to her was, 'You aren't hurt, are you? You walked straight into the car. I called out to you and you didn't hear.'

She blinked back at him, wondering why she should be lying on her back in the road, and remembering suddenly stepping off the pavement into nothing, and she said, 'I always forget to look where I am going.'

Then he laughed, and said, 'You silly one,' brushing the dust from her skirt, while she watched him gravely, aware, with a little sick sensation, 'this has happened before.' She turned towards the car and it seemed to her that she recognised the set of his shoulders and the way his hair grew at the back of his head. His hands, brown and capable, they were the hands she knew. Yet her eyes could not deceive her and she had never seen him before.

'You look pale and shaken,' he said, 'I'm going to drive you home: tell me where it is,' and she climbed in beside him, knowing that the pallor of her face was nothing to do with the accident nor her recent illness: she was white from the shock of seeing him, and the realisation that this was the beginning of things and the cycle had begun. Then her fragment of knowledge was gone from her, like the dream that departed at daybreak, and they were a man and a woman unknown to one another, talking of trivialities, glad in each other's company. She was telling him,

'It's not very pretty this part of the world, just suburbs, not real country,' and he smiled and said, 'All country except the west seems foreign to me and dull; but then I come from Ryeshire.'

'Ryeshire,' she echoed, 'No, I've never been as far as that,' and she lingered over the word, repeating it, as though it found response in her heart like a lost chord. 'I've lived here all my life,' she said, and the words trailed away like words belonging to someone else, someone left behind, a younger sister, and she herself wandering through a field of sorrel with the scent of honeysuckle in her nostrils and the sound of a river in her ears, born anew, alive for the first time.

She heard herself saying, 'I remember Ryeshire was coloured yellow in my atlas in school,' and he laughed: 'What a funny thing to remember.' Then again came the flash of knowledge: 'He'll tease me about that one day and I shall look back at this moment.' She must remind herself that they were strangers, none of that had happened, and she was only a girl who had been ill, who was dull, who was absent-minded, and 'Would you like some tea?' she said, formal and polite. 'I think we shall find my aunt at home.'

The patter of conversation, the crunch of toast, the maid coming in to light the lamps, the dog begging for sugar, these were natural, inevitable things; but they held significance, as if they were pictures hanging on a wall and she were a visitor to a gallery inspecting each picture in turn. And later: 'Good-bye,' she said, knowing she would see him again and glad at the thought, but something inside her afraid of the knowledge, wanting to thrust it aside.

That night she saw the valley very clearly; she climbed the path to the house and stood on the terrace outside the open window, and it seemed to her that the old sensation of peace and escape from the world was intermingled now with a new consciousness that the house was no longer empty, it was tenanted, it held a welcome. She tried to reach to the window but the effort was too much for her, her arms fell to her side, the image dissolved, and she was staring with wide-awake eyes at the door of her own bedroom. She was aware that it was still very early, the maids not yet astir, but the telephone was ringing in the hall.

She went downstairs and took off the receiver, and it was his voice. He was saying, 'Please forgive me. I know that it's an impossible hour to ring up, but I've just had the most vivid nightmare that something had happened to you.' He tried to laugh, ashamed of his weakness. 'It was so strong, I can scarcely believe now it isn't true.'

'I'm perfectly all right,' she said, and she laughed back at him. 'I was sleeping very peacefully and feeling happy. Your ringing must have awakened me. What did you think was the matter?'

'I can't explain,' he said, and his voice was puzzled. 'I was certain you had gone away and were never coming back. It was quite definite, you had gone away for good. There was no possible means of getting in touch with you. You had gone away on your own accord.'

'Well, it's not true,' she said, smiling at his distress, 'I'm here, quite safe – but it was nice of you to mind.'

'I want to see you to-day,' he insisted, 'just to make sure that nothing has happened. That you still look the same. You see, it's my fault, if I hadn't knocked you down with the car this wouldn't have happened . . . That's what I felt,

151

all mixed up in the nightmare. You will let me see you; tell me you will?'

'Yes,' she said. 'Yes, I'd like to see you too,' because it had to happen, she had no choice, and his voice was the echo of her own thoughts, suppressed and unfulfilled.

When they were married, he used to tease her about that first morning after they had met, and how his telephoning had roused her from her sleep. 'You can't escape now,' he said, 'you belong to me and are safe for eternity. My nightmare was indigestion. You must have been in love with me to have answered the telephone so promptly! Look at me, what are you thinking about? Mooning again, always mooning.'

He put his arm round her and kissed the top of her head, and although she clung to him in response there was a little pang in her heart because after all perhaps he had not understood; he would be like the rest of the world, irritated in spite of himself at her abstraction. 'I don't moon,' she said, leaning against his shoulder, aware that she loved him, but part of her still unclaimed, inviolate, that he could not touch, and for all her worship of his hands, his voice, his presence, she wanted to creep away, be silent, be at rest.

They stood at the window of the little inn looking down on the river, the rocking boats, and the distant woods beyond. 'You're happy, aren't you?' he said, 'and Ryeshire is as lovely as you expected, isn't it?'

'Much lovelier,' she told him.

'Better than the yellow corner of your atlas?' he laughed. 'Listen, to-morrow we'll explore, we'll wander over the hills, we'll plunge into the woods.' He spread his map upon the table, he busied himself with plans and a guide of the district. She felt restless, stirred by a strange energy. She wanted to be out, to be walking, not idling here in the little sitting-room. 'Some time I must clean the car and fill up with petrol,' he said, 'stroll up the road and I'll follow later. I won't be long.'

She slipped out of the inn, and up the road to the bend of the river, then down to the beach, stumbling over stones and seaweed and little loose boulders of rock. She came to a creek turning westward, surrounded on either side by trees sloping to the water's edge. There were no boats in this creek; it was silent and still, the quiet broken once by the movement of a fish below the surface casting a ripple on the face of the water. Now the beach vanished into the coming tide and she must force her way through the trees to the high ground above, plunging steadily, excited for no known reason, feeling that the very silence was due to her, and the trees rustled in homage, dark and green, the outposts of enchantment.

Suddenly the path dipped, and she was taken down, down, into the confusion of a valley, her valley, the place where she belonged. The tall beech trees were on either side, and then, as she had always known it, the path dwindling to a mud track, tangled and overgrown, while yonder the house waited, mysterious and hushed, the wide windows alight as though afire with the rays of the setting sun, beautiful, expect-ant. She knew she was not frightened at the realisation of her dream, it was the embodiment of peace, like the answer to a prayer. At first glance the place had seemed deserted and the house untenanted, but as she came on to the terrace it was as though the white walls flushed somehow and were strengthened, and what she had thought were weeds forcing themselves through the crazy paving were rock plants in bloom. She felt a pang of disappointment that her house should be the dwelling-place of other people. She crept closer, and raising her arms to the sill – always the final action in her dream – she gazed through the window to the room beyond. The room was cool and filled with flowers, the warm sun did not touch the coloured chintzes. It was a gay room, a boy's room, the only formal note the heavy chandelier hanging from the ceiling.

There was a table in the middle with a butterfly net on it, story-books lying on the chairs, and in the corner of the sofa a bow and arrow with a piece of broken string. A jersey was hanging from a hook on the door, and the door was open as though someone had just left the room. She leant with her cheek against the sill, rested and happy, and she was thinking 'I'd like to know the boy who lives here.' As she smiled, idle and content, her eyes fell upon a photograph on the mantelpiece, and she saw that it was a photograph of herself. One that she did not know, with her hair done differently, a likeness which, with all its fresh-ness and modernity, struck her as being in contrast to the room curiously faded and old-fashioned.

'It's a joke,' she thought, bewildered, 'someone knew I was coming and put it there for fun.' Then she saw her husband's pipe on the mantelpiece, the one with the knobbly bowl, and above, the old sporting print that her aunt had given her. The furniture, the pictures, she was intimate with them all, they belonged to her. Yet she knew these things were waiting in packing cases in her aunt's house in Middlesex and they could not be here. She felt nervous and distressed, she knew not why, and 'It's a silly sort of joke,' she thought, 'he is making fun of my dream.' But, puzzled, she hesitated, her husband did not know about the dream. Then she heard a step, and he came into the room. He seemed very tired, as though he had been searching for her a long time, and had come to the house by a different way. He looked strange, too; he had parted his hair and changed his suit.

'What's the matter?' she said, 'how did you get here? Do you know the people who live in the house?' He did not hear her, but sat down on the sofa and picked up a paper. 'Don't pretend any more,' she said, 'look at me, darling, laugh at me, tell me what has happened, what are you doing here?'

He took no notice, and then a manservant came in and began to lay tea on the table in the middle. 'The sun's in my eyes,' said her husband, 'will you pull down the blind?' and the man came forward and jerked at the curtains, staring straight at her without recognition, ignoring her as his master had done, and the curtains were drawn so that she could not see them any more. A moment later she heard the sound of a gong.

She felt very tired suddenly, very weak, as though life were too much for her, too difficult, more than she could ever bear: she wanted to cry, and 'If only I could rest I wouldn't mind,' she thought, 'but it's such a silly joke . . .' and she turned away from the window and looked down the path to the tangled valley below, exquisitely scented, mysterious and deep. There would be moss there, soft bracken, the cool foliage of trees, and the lilting murmur of a brook singing in her ears. She would find a resting place there where they could not tease her, she would crouch there and hide, and presently he would reproach himself for having frightened her, and would come out on to the terrace and call down to her.

155

As she hesitated at the top of the path, she saw a small boy staring at her from the bushes who had not been there before. His eyes were large and brown like buttons in his face, and there was a large scratch on his cheek. She felt shy, wondering how long he had been watching her. 'Everyone seems to be playing hide-and-seek here,' she said. 'I can't make it out, they pretend they don't see me.'

He smiled, biting his nails. She wanted to touch him; he was dear for no reason; but he was nervous like a startled fawn and edged away. 'Don't be afraid,' she said gently, 'I won't hurt you. I want to go down into the valley, will you come with me?'

She held out her hand, but he backed, shaking his head, red in the face, so she set off alone, with him trotting some distance behind, peering at her, still uncertain of her, still scared. The trees closed in upon them and the shadows, the song of the brook rang near, and she hummed to herself, lighthearted and happy. They came to a clearing in the trees and a bank of moss beside the stream. 'How lovely,' she thought. 'How peaceful, they'll never find me here,' delighted with the mischief she had planned, when the boy's voice, quiet as a whisper, came to her for the first time.

'Take care,' he was saying, 'Take care, you're standing on the grave.'

'What do you mean?' she said, and looked down at her feet, but there was only moss beneath her: the stems of bracken, and the crushed head of a blue hydrangea flower. 'Whose grave?' she said, raising her head. Only he was not there any more: there was no boy, he was gone, and his voice was an echo. She called him: 'Are you hiding? Where are you?' and there was no answer. She ran back along the path to the house, out of the shadows, and she could not find him.

'Come back, don't be frightened; where are you?' she called, and then came once more upon the terrace by the house. With a little sense of fear in her heart she saw that the white walls of the house no longer glowed in the warmth of the sun. There were weeds between the paving, not plants as she had thought. There were no curtains on the window of the room, and the room was empty, the walls unpapered, the floors bare boards.

Only the gaunt chandelier hung from the ceiling, grimy with cobwebs, and a breeze blew through the open window so that it swung very gently like the pendulum of a clock, to and fro, ticking out time. Then she turned and ran fast along the path whence she had come, up and away from the silence and the shadows, running from this place that was unreal, untrue, so desolate, forlorn. Only herself was real, and the great murky ball of the sun setting between the beech-trees at the head of the avenue, hard and red, like a flaming lamp.

He found her wandering up and down the beach by the river, staring before her, crying to herself. 'But what is it, my darling?' he kept saying. 'Did you fall, are you hurt?' She clung to him, clutching the safety of his coat.

'I don't know,' she whispered, 'I don't know. I can't remember. I went for a walk in a wood somewhere, and I forget what happened. I keep feeling I've lost something and I don't know what it is.'

'You silly one,' he said, 'you silly, mooning one, I must look after you better. Stop crying, there's no reason to cry. Come indoors, I've got a surprise for you.'

They went into the inn and he made her sit beside him in the chair. 'I've got a lovely idea, and it's going to thrill you. I've been talking to the landlord of the inn,' he said, his cheek against her hair. 'He tells me there's a property near here for sale, a lovely old manor house, a place after your own heart. Been empty for years, just waiting for people like us. Would you like to live in this part of the world?' She nodded, content once more, smiling up at him, the memory of what had been gone from her.

'Look, I'll show you on the map,' he said, 'here's the house and there's the garden, right in the hollow, running down to the creek. There's a stream about here, and a clearing place in the trees, a place for you, beloved, where you can wander, and rest, and be alone. It's wild and tangled, quite overgrown in parts; they call it the Happy Valley.'

And His Letters Grew Colder

Dear Mrs B:

Forgive me writing to you like this without the slightest introduction. The fact is, I know your brother out in China, and having successfully wangled six months' furlough, arriving in England a few days ago, I am seizing this opportunity to tell you how very pleased I should be if you would let me look you up sometime and give you news of Charlie. He is extremely fit, and sends you many messages, of course.

Please excuse me for blundering in upon you in this abrupt manner. I am,
Yours sincerely,
X.Y.Z.

June the fourth

Dear Mrs B:

I shall be delighted to come to your cocktail party on Friday. It is very charming of you to ask me.
Yours sincerely,
X.Y.Z.

June the seventh

Dear Mrs B:

I cannot let the day pass without telling you how much I enjoyed your party yesterday, and the very great pleasure I had in meeting you. I must have appeared horribly gauche and awkward, for I am afraid three years in China have played the deuce with my manners and my conversation! You were so sweet and kind to me, and I am certain I babbled a great deal of incoherent nonsense.

It is a little bewildering to find oneself back in civilisation, and in the company of a woman of your beauty and intelligence. Now I have said too much! Do you really mean I may come to see you again soon?
Yours very sincerely,
X. Y. Z.

June the tenth
Dear Mrs B:
I shall certainly accept your invitation to dine this evening. Will you excuse my poor bridge?
Yours,
X.Y.Z.

June the twelfth
Dear Mrs B:
I have taken you at your word and have secured a couple of seats for that revue you wanted to see. You won't break your promise about coming, will you? If you care about it, we might go on to supper somewhere afterwards and dance.
X.Y.Z.

Dear A,

Do you really mean I may call you A? And did
you mean one or two other things you said last
night? Whether you meant them or not, I want to
thank you for a marvellous evening. I was so
happy, I don't believe I ever apologised for my
atrocious dancing!
Thank you.
X

June the seventeenth
Dear A,

Sorry! I know I behaved like a bear on the
telephone, but I was so wretchedly disappointed
that you could not manage to come out, after all.
Will you ever forgive me? Of course I understand.
May I come round some time tomorrow?
X

June the nineteenth
I'm glad you put me off that evening, because if
you hadn't rung me up to tell me so, and if I
hadn't been rude over the telephone, then I should
never have come round to see you this afternoon.

Why were you so wonderful to me? Perhaps
you were merely taking pity on a poor dull dog
arrived from the ends of the earth! I don't think
ever in my life I have been able to talk to anyone
as I have to you.

You made me feel as though things really are
worth while; that there is more to look forward to

in life than a dreary plantation surrounded by coolies. D'you know, I'll make a confession to you. Out in China I used to go to Charlie's place merely to look at the photograph of you that he had hanging over his desk.

In a way, I believe I idolised it; I could not believe that there really existed anyone so lovely. And then, when I came over here and knew I was going to meet you for the first time, I felt as nervous and shy as any schoolboy. I was so terrified that my photograph was going to be spoiled in some way.

When I saw you – well, I could go on for pages and pages just describing how you looked and what I felt. But what's the use? You would probably throw it unread into the wastepaper basket, and who would blame you! No; I shall do my best not to bore you in that way. You must be sick and tired of all the men who tell you you are beautiful. Can we be friends, though – real friends?

X

June the twenty-second

My dear,

I explained myself badly on the telephone this morning. I called round at once after you rang off, but your maid told me you had already gone out. So I am writing this note instead. You did not understand what I meant about this evening. It's only that it's so marvellous talking to you that I feel as though the hours were somehow wasted by going to a theatre!

Yes, I agree; I am idiotic and unreasonable.

162

Somehow, I had imagined us dining somewhere quietly in Soho – and then perhaps going back to your house. But of course I will do anything you want.

Incidentally, I forgot to tell you that I am moving from this hotel. The service is bad and there seems to be no privacy. I'm thinking of taking a furnished apartment. But we will talk about that this evening. You aren't angry with me, are you?

X

June the twenty-third

A,

What am I to say? What can you think of me? I am so desperately ashamed of myself. No; there is no excuse, of course. I must have been mad . . . I never went back to the hotel after I left you. I've been walking about all night, miserable and out of my mind.

It is impossible for you to imagine my agony of reproach. I don't know if for one moment you can understand what it means for someone who has spent three lonely, uncivilised years, living like a savage among other savages, to find himself all at once treated as a human being by a lovely and adorable woman like yourself. It proved too much for me – too intoxicating.

Yes, I lost my head; I behaved as I should never dreamed it possible that I could behave. Can't you see how difficult you made it for me? No; how should you? You were gentle; you were wonderful;

163

you were you. I am to blame entirely. I will do any mortal thing if only you will try to forget what I said.

I swear to you solemnly by all I hold most dear that I will never make love to you again. Never . . . never . . . We will start once more at the beginning. My dear, I want to be your friend: somebody you feel you can trust; someone with whom you can relax, with whom you need make no effort.

Words . . . words . . . How can I explain? A, is there a chance of my being forgiven? A word from you will rouse me from my present depths of desolation. I shall be waiting all day, in case. Forgive me.

X

June the twenty-fifth

When I heard your voice on the telephone, I trembled so that I could hardly answer! Absurd, isn't it?

But none of that matters now. The only thing that matters is that you have forgiven me, and we are friends again. It is all right, isn't it? We are friends, aren't we? Yes: let's drive into the country tomorrow to some little place miles from anywhere, and talk and talk. I have so much to tell you.

Bless you,

X

June the twenty-seventh

A, here are some flowers for you in memory of
yesterday. I wonder if you have the remotest idea
of what the day meant to me! You said you loved
it too. Did you? I can't forget that little inn by
the side of the water, and how we sat there
dreaming.

I'm so glad the country appeals to you as it
does to me. You know, we think alike in most
things. In some ways, my dear, your brain is most
extraordinarily like that of a man. You see straight;
you don't muddle your ideas – and you have such
a sense of values. And then on the other hand,
you are perhaps the most feminine person
imaginable.

I have taken the apartment I told you about.
The sitting room wants only one thing now –
your photograph. You promised me one days ago.

Yes, I'll call for you this evening at ten, and
we'll go some place and dance. It will be perfect,
of course. Wear your green dress, will you? I saw
some beads exactly that colour. May I bring them
for you?

X

July the first

A, darling, it's no good, I couldn't help myself. You
looked so lovely. I'm not made of iron, but flesh
and blood. What am I going to do about it?

I value your friendship more than anything in
the world, but why aren't you old and ugly? It
would be so much easier for me.

165

You like me a little bit, don't you? Or don't you? I don't know what I'm writing.

When am I going to see you?

X

My darling, you made me so absurdly happy last night. I can't believe they are true – the things you said. You told me you liked orchids. Here are all the orchids I could find.

I'll rob every hothouse in England if you want me to. I'll do anything you want, give you anything you want – if only you'll let me see you every day.

I won't ask for much in return – just to be allowed to sit at your feet and worship. Nothing more than that.

You're lovely, lovely, lovely.

X

I can't exist like this. I tell you it's impossible. You're driving me insane. You let me see you, and then you expect me to stand like a dummy without senses.

I've been at the telephone all day and have had no answer from you. Where were you and whom were you with?

Oh! Yes, laugh at me, I don't care. Of course, I agree I have no right to ask you questions. You are perfectly free. When you laugh like that I want to strangle you – and then I want to love you.

I must see you.

X

July the eighth
3 A.M.

Beloved,

It's absurd to write to you, isn't it, after this evening? The room is full of you still. I can't think of anything else. I know now that I have been waiting all my life for this. Sleep well. God bless you. Take care of yourself.

Do you love me?

X

July the ninth

Sweet,

Of course it's all right. Expecting you this afternoon between five and six.

X

July the tenth

My darling,

No: come tomorrow. You must, you must! I can't wait for you until Saturday, not after yesterday.

Couldn't we possibly lunch somewhere first, and then come back here afterwards?

Please! I love you so much.

X

July the fifteenth

Beloved,

Your maid answered the telephone this morning
when you were out, so I disguised my voice and
gave another name.

Couldn't we go out into the country? You
remember that little place we went to in June, by
the water? Then after luncheon we could stroll in
those woods . . . They look very lonely and
deserted.

Say yes, will you? Telephone me and we'll
arrange to meet somewhere. I had better not pick
you up.

Your

X

July the nineteenth

What about four o'clock?

X

July the twentieth

My dearest,

I think we had better go to the other place, it's
quieter. Besides, there are two entrances. What bad
luck, your knowing the fellow who lives here in
the same block! We'll have to be careful.

X

July the twenty-first

Angel,

Very well; I'll pick you up tomorrow outside
your club. Leave the car parked outside with the

168

hood up, and I'll sit inside and wait for you. I suggest we go to the country again. There's less chance of running across anyone.

By the way, I've found out that the fellow you know is out all day, doesn't get back until the evening, so we needn't worry about him when we're at the apartment.

I don't know how to wait until tomorrow.

You know that question you asked me? The answer is Yes — a thousand times! You are *adorable*!
X

July the twenty-fifth

Yes, I know I was nervy and irritable today. You must forgive me. But seeing you as I do, at odd hours, makes me dissatisfied. I don't know. It's as though I wanted to be with you all the time. Couldn't we go away somewhere, for the weekend? Some place where we could be by ourselves.

We would be very careful; no one need ever find out. What do you think, my sweet?
Your
X

July the twenty-seventh

Angel,

But you are marvellous! What a brilliant idea! I should never have thought of a sick friend in Devonshire! Yes; you can rely on me to be discreet. I'll be at Paddington at a quarter to eleven.
X

169

August the fifth

My beloved Sweet,

I haven't dared ring you up in case it should seem odd. These few days with you have been so marvellous, so utterly unspeakable. Darling, I don't know how I am going to go on as we did before.

Those wretched, hurried meetings after the hours we spent together. I'm so happy and so miserable. I'll wait at the apartment all day in case you should come.

Your own

X

August the seventh

Yesterday was *heaven*. What time tomorrow? I think the afternoons are safest.

X

August the twelfth

Dearest,

What about suggesting your idea and seeing how it is taken? After all, if you are in the habit of going to Aix every year for this cure, why should it look strange suddenly? You can say you are tired of Aix itself and have heard of a smaller place just as good but not nearly so expensive. That is sure to go well!

You see, sweet, I could go out there about the nineteenth and you could join me a few days later. I think that would be the wisest plan.

170

Anyway, there's no harm in trying, and you can tell me tomorrow what happened.

See you after seven.

X

August the fourteenth

My own,

To think that it will really come true – that we shall be together night and day for three weeks, perhaps a month. It's too wonderful, my precious; it's like a dream out of which one will be wakened suddenly.

Tell me you are happy, too. Hours and hours of each other, and nothing to separate us. I'm never going to stop loving you for one single instant.

Your very own,

X

August the twentieth

I'm just off, sweet. I'm so excited! Three days of agony until you follow me South – and then . . .

X

September the twenty-sixth

Darling,

I arrived back in town about two hours ago. I can scarcely believe we've been away a month.
Sometimes it seems a day; sometimes it seems a year.

Thank you for your sweet letter, darling. When am I going to see you?

X

September the twenty-ninth

My darling,

It was lovely being with you all yesterday. It was almost as though we were down in the South again.

And the little inn by the river was just the same as ever, wasn't it?

Now, dearest, about our seeing each other. We must be terribly careful because if our names get coupled and people start talking, and it all came out about our being away together – well, you can imagine what would happen. We had better go very slowly at first. You do understand, don't you? It's all for your sake.

X

October the fourth

Yes darling, come along if you like between six and seven, but do remember not to bring the car. Sorry about not having telephoned. I thought it safer.

X

October the ninth

Dearest,

Wouldn't you rather do a theatre and dance afterwards than spend the evening here? I mean, there's always the chance of your being seen.

I've heard the new Wallace play is a thrill. What do you say? Let me know so that I can get seats.

X

October the twelfth

Sweetheart,

You mustn't be so unreasonable. You don't seem to understand what the consequences would be if we were found out. I've thought it all over very carefully from every angle, and it would be hopeless – quite hopeless. Life wouldn't be worth living for either of us.

You know I want to see you as much as you want to see me, but it's no use running into danger. You were in a difficult mood yesterday, and deliberately misunderstood every word I said. I don't mean to be hard, but you do see, don't you? Come for luncheon tomorrow and we'll talk over plans. All love,

X

October the sixteenth

Sorry, darling, I was out when you telephoned, and didn't get back till late so couldn't ring you. Was your message for dinner on Thursday? I can't manage Thursday, darling. What about Friday afternoon? We might go to a picture.

Do remember to ring me up from your club and not from your house. Servants might be listening. Haven't you any sense of discretion? See you soon.

X

                              October the twenty-fourth
Darling,

Don't you realise it would be madness to go
away for the week-end? Surely we've been over
that question time and time again. We've only to
take a wrong turn and the whole affair is broadcast
to the world. To say we did so in July is no answer
to the present argument.

It's absurd to say I'm different. I'm just the
same as ever. I wish you wouldn't be so feminine
and unreasonable. You don't see straight at all,
darling.

By the way, the price they asked for that
necklace was sheer robbery. Perhaps we can find
something else. I'll ring you up at the end of the
week.
X

                              October the twenty-ninth
Isn't it rather cold for the country? Let's have
luncheon Saturday instead.
X

                              October the thirty-first
Here are some chrysanthemums for you. Of course
I love you. But you mustn't behave in that absurd
way again, darling, or I shall be very angry. I can't
bear scenes. See you Monday.
X

November the fifth

Darling,

I'm afraid this week is very difficult. I've got
loads of things that must be done. I might be able
to snatch an hour on Thursday. Keep the afternoon
free.

In haste,

X

November the ninth

My dear,

Why must you spoil everything? I was perfectly
ready to enjoy our afternoon together, and you
needs must cross-question me as though you
expected every word I said to be a lie.

Sometimes I don't think you have ever
understood me at all. What's to be the outcome of
it? Is it always to be this incessant quarrelling
whenever we meet? It looks that way, doesn't it?

And why this new thing of jealousy? It's
ridiculous and nerve-wracking. Can't we be friends
without all this nonsense?

X

November the thirteenth

All right. Wednesday at one. But don't come to the
apartment. I'll meet you at the Savoy.

X

November the sixteenth

Just a line to say I can't manage tomorrow night,

after all. So sorry not to let you know before. Will ring the club tomorrow.

X

November the eighteenth

A, dear,

I should be glad if you would cease spying on my movements. If I chose to spend the evening talking business with a friend it's my affair entirely. Remember this once and for all. Aren't you making yourself slightly ridiculous?

Yours,

X

November the twentieth

My dear A,

I received your extremely incoherent message on the telephone but scarcely know what it is all about. I accept your apologies, but need we go into that?

About seeing you – I can't definitely say when. I have so many things to see to. I will try to let you know.

X

November the twenty-fourth

Dear A,

How ridiculous you are! As if I should disguise my voice on the telephone. It was the servant who answered. I was out all day. No, I'm afraid I shan't be able to see you this evening. I'll let you know when I can.

X

Dear A,

Why not be frank with yourself and admit that it isn't because you have messages to send to Charles that you want to see me? I know only too well that it will mean another scene of reproach, more tears, more nerves.

I've had enough. Can't you realise that it's finished? I shan't be able to breathe until I get out of this over-civilised, oversexed country, back to the peace and security of my plantation.

Now you know the truth.

Good-by.

X

Telephone message sent December first to Mrs B:
'Mr X.Y.Z. sailed for China today.'

The Limpet

No one can call me an insensitive woman. That has been my trouble. If I could harden myself to other people's feelings, life would be very different. As it is, here I am today a positive wreck, and through no fault of my own, but just because I can't bear to hurt the people I love.

What is the future to be? I ask myself the question a hundred times a day. I'm nearly forty, my looks are going, and if my health goes too – which wouldn't surprise me, after all I've been through – then I shall have to give up this job and live on the ridiculous alimony that I get from Kenneth. A fine outlook.

Well, there's one thing. I keep my sense of humour. My friends, the few I have, give me credit for that at least. And they say I'm plucky. They ought to see me sometimes. When I come back from work at the end of the day (and often it's after seven before I get home – my boss has no tender feelings, I can tell you that much), I have my little bit of supper to get. Then there's the flat to dust and put straight – the woman who comes in twice a week always leaves something in the wrong place. Coming on top of a heavy day, by this time I'm so exhausted that I just feel like throwing myself on my bed and ending it all.

Then perhaps the telephone rings, and I make the most

tremendous effort to be bright. Sometimes I catch a glimpse of myself in the looking glass – sixty-five if I'm a day, with those dreary lines, and my hair's lost its colour too. As often as not it's some woman friend cancelling lunch on Sunday because she has something better to do, or my mother-in-law complaining of her bronchitis or the letter she's had from Kenneth – as if that's my concern these days. The point is that none of them consider my feelings in the way I consider theirs.

I'm the one to get what Father used to call 'the thick end of the stick', and it's been like that for as long as I can remember, way back in the days when he and Mother used to squabble like cat and dog and I had to play the part of go-between. I don't pretend to have brains – I never have had. Plenty of common sense when dealing with everyday matters, and I've never been sacked from a job yet – I've always been the one to hand in the notice. But when it comes to asking for anything for myself, or sticking up for my own rights, as I should have done with Kenneth, then I'm quite hopeless. I just give in and say nothing. I suppose I've been more put upon in life, more used, more hurt, than anyone would credit could be possible for one lone woman. Call it fate or misfortune, call it what you will, it's true.

And it comes from being unselfish, though I say it myself. Take what happened recently. I could have married Edward any time during the past three years, but I always refused to do anything drastic, for his sake. You have a wife and a career, I used to say to him, and your duty is to put them first. Silly, I dare say. I can't think of any other woman who would have behaved in that way. But then I have my ideals, and certain things are right and certain things are wrong. I inherited that from Father.

When Kenneth left me – and I'd been through hell for six years – I didn't go round complaining to all his friends. I just said we were incompatible, and his restless temperament clashed with my own more stay-at-home nature, and all that whisky drinking was not the happiest way to start a family. For a woman whose health has always been tricky he asked a lot, what with keeping him going while he had the drinking bouts, and cooking for him, and cleaning the flat, hardly able to stand myself – well, I said to his friends, it seemed really wiser to let him go. I collapsed afterwards, of course. Flesh and blood could bear no more. But blame him . . . no. It's far more dignified to keep silent when one is lacerated.

The first time I realised how much people were going to depend on me in life was when Father and Mother came to me in turn about their own troubles. I was only fourteen at the time. We were living in Eastbourne. My father was in a solicitor's office, not exactly a partner in the firm, but in an important position above the head clerk, and my mother looked after the house. It was quite a nice house, standing in its own garden, not semidetached or anything of that sort, and we kept a general maid.

Being an only child, I suppose I got into the habit of listening too much to grown-up conversation. I remember so well coming back from school wearing my little gym dress with the white-flannel shirt, and carrying the ugly school hat slung on my back. I stood in the hall, pulling off my shoes outside the dining-room – we used the dining-room as a living-room in winter, because the drawing-room faced north – and I heard Father say, 'What *are* we going to say to Dilly?' Dilys is such a pretty name, too, but they always called me Dilly.

I knew at once that something was wrong, from the very tone of Father's voice and the emphasis on the 'are', as if they were in some sort of quandary. Well, any other child would either have taken no notice and forgotten about it, or walked straight in and said there and then, 'What's wrong?' I was far too sensitive for that. I stood outside the dining-room, trying to hear what my mother answered, but all I could catch was something about, 'She'll soon settle down.' Then I heard movement as if she was getting up from her chair, so I quickly ran upstairs. Something was afoot, some change, which was going to make a difference to all our lives, and from the way Mother said, 'She'll soon settle down,' it sounded as if they were doubtful how I should take it.

Now, I've never been strong, and as a child I used to catch the most appalling colds. I was at the tail end of one on that particular evening, and somehow hearing the whispered voices seemed to bring the cold back again. I had to keep blowing and blowing my nose up in that cold little bedroom of mine, so that when I went downstairs my poor eyes and nose were red and swollen, and I must have looked a miserable sight.

'Oh, Dilly,' said my mother, 'whatever's the matter? Is your cold worse?' And Father stared at me, too, in great concern.

'It's nothing,' I told them. 'I just haven't felt very well all day, and I've been working rather hard on the exams for the end of term.'

Then suddenly – I couldn't stop myself – I burst into tears. There was silence from Father and Mother, but they both looked very uncomfortable and worried, and I saw them exchange glances.

'You ought to be in bed, dear,' said Mother. 'Why not go up, and I'll bring you your supper on a tray?'

Then – it just shows how sensitive I was – I jumped up and ran round to her and put my arms about her, and I said, 'If anything ever happened to you and Father, I should die!'

That was all. Nothing more. Then I smiled, and wiped my eyes, and said, 'I'm going to wait on you for a change. I'll get the supper.' And I wouldn't hear of Mother helping me; I was determined to show how useful I could be.

That night my father came and sat on my bed and told me about the job he had been offered in Australia, and how if he went it would mean leaving me behind for the first year, while he and Mother got settled in and found a home for the three of us. I didn't attempt to cry or make any sort of fuss. I just nodded my head and said, 'You've got to do what you think is best. You mustn't consider me.'

'That's all very well,' he answered, 'but we can't go off and leave you at boarding school unless we are quite satisfied you're going to be happy, and that you'll make the best of it with your Aunt Madge.' This was his sister, who lived in London.

'Of course I'll make the best of it,' I said. 'And I'll soon get used to being on my own. It may be a bit hard at first, because Aunt Madge has never cared twopence for me, and I know she has heaps of friends and likes going out in the evenings, which will mean I shall be left in that draughty old house by myself. Still, I can write to you and Mother every day during the holidays, and then I shan't feel so cut off, and at school I shall be working so hard there won't be time to think.'

183

I remember he looked a bit upset – poor old Father, he was sensitive like me – and he said, 'What makes you say that about your aunt?'

'Nothing definite,' I told him. 'It's just her manner and the way she's always been down on me. But don't let it worry you. I suppose I can take my own little possessions and have them in my bedroom there? It would mean a link with all the things I love.'

He got up and walked about the room. Then he said, 'It's not absolutely settled, you know. I've promised the firm I'll think it over.'

I wasn't going to show him I minded, so I lay back in bed and hid my face in the blanket and said, 'If you really and truly think you and Mother will be happy in Australia, you've got to go.'

I was peeping over the blanket and I can see his expression now. His face was all puckered up and distressed, which made me quite certain that, if he did go to Australia, it would be a big mistake.

The next morning my cold was worse, and Mother tried to make me stay in bed, but I insisted on getting up and going off to school as usual.

'I can't go on making a fuss about a silly cold,' I told her. 'I've got to harden up, in future, and try to forget how you and Father have spoilt me. Aunt Madge will think me an awful nuisance if I expect to stay in bed whenever I have a cold. What with London fogs, and so on, I shall probably have a cold the whole winter, so I may as well become used to it.' And I laughed cheerfully, so as not to worry her, and teased her too, and said how lovely it would be for her in the warm sunshine of Australia, while I was sitting alone in the bedroom of Aunt Madge's London house.

'You know we'd take you with us if we could,' said Mother. 'But it's the fare, for one thing, and not being quite certain what we shall find when we get there.'

'I know,' I said. 'That's what's worrying Father, isn't it, the uncertainty of it, going to a life he doesn't know, and cutting himself off from all his old ties here.'

'Did he tell you that?' Mother asked me.

'No, but I could feel it,' I said. 'It's a wrench, and he won't admit it.'

Father had already left for the office, so we were alone, Mother and I. The maid was busy with the bedrooms upstairs, and I was stuffing my school things into my satchel.

'I thought he seemed so happy about it all,' said Mother. 'He was really excited when we first discussed the plan.'

'Well, you know best,' I said, 'but Father's always been like that, hasn't he? Wild over something at first, and then he cools off when it's too late, like the time he bought that motor mower and you had to go without a winter coat. It would be terrible if you got out there and he found he didn't settle happily after all.'

'Yes,' said Mother, 'yes, I know . . . I admit I wasn't enthusiastic myself at first, but he talked me round.'

It was time for me to catch the bus to school, so I didn't discuss it any more, but to show how much I sympathised I hugged her very hard, and said, 'I do hope so much you're going to be happy and that you'll enjoy the business of hunting for a house and running it all yourself. You'll miss Florence at first' – Florence was our maid, she'd been with us a long time – 'and I know it's hard to find help in Australia. One of the mistresses at school is an Australian, and it's a great place for young people but not for the middle-aged, according to her. But then, that

185

will be part of the excitement, won't it, being a pioneer, and living rough.'

I blew my nose again, because of the wretched cold, and left her to finish her breakfast, but I could see she wasn't all that happy about Australia, not deep down.

Well, the long and the short of it was, they never went in the end. I don't know to this day why it was, but I think it must have been because they both depended on me so much that they couldn't bear to part with me, even for a year.

It's a funny thing, but after that time, after the Australia plan was shelved, I mean, Father and Mother seemed to drift apart, and Father began to lose interest in life, and in his work, too. He used to nag at Mother, and Mother would nag at him, and I found myself acting the part of peacemaker. Father took to staying out in the evening, at his club, so he said, and often I remember Mother would say to me with a sigh, 'Your father's late again. I wonder what's kept him tonight?'

I would look up from my homework and say – just to tease, you know – 'You shouldn't have married a man younger than yourself. He likes young company, that's what it is, and he finds it with those girls in the office, not all that older than I am myself.'

Mother didn't make the best of herself, it was true. She was such a home bird, always in and out of the kitchen, making pastry and cakes, which she did so much better than Florence. I've inherited that from her, I'm glad to say – no one can teach me anything about cooking. But, of course, it meant she was apt to neglect her appearance. Then, when Father finally did come in, I would creep out into the hall to meet him, and make a face, and put my finger to my lips.

'You're in disgrace,' I would whisper. 'Mother's been on about it half the evening. Just come in and read the paper and don't say anything.'

Poor Father, he immediately looked guilty, and there would be a fine evening in front of us, with Mother tight-lipped at her end of the table, and he sulky at his, and me between the pair of them trying to do the best for both.

When I left school the question arose, what was I to do? I've told you I had no brains, but I was quick, and fairly bright in the ordinary things, so I took a typing and shorthand course, and thank heaven I did, as events turned out. At the time I didn't think it would lead to anything. I was eighteen then, and, like most girls of my age, stage-struck. I had taken a leading part in *The School for Scandal* at school, played Lady Teazle, as a matter of fact, and could think of nothing else – the reporter was a friend of the headmistress, and I got a mention in the local paper – but when I suggested going on the stage both Father and Mother put their foot down.

'You don't know the first way to set about it,' said Father, 'apart from the cost of the training.'

'Besides,' said Mother, 'it would mean living up in London and being on your own. It would never do!'

I took the secretarial course just to have it up my sleeve, but I hadn't given up all thoughts of the stage. The way I saw things, there was no future for any of us living in Eastbourne. There was Father still dug in at the solicitor's office, and Mother pottering about at home; it was so narrowing to their outlook that they seemed to get nothing out of life. Whereas if they went up to London to live, there would be a mass of new interests for them. Father would enjoy the football matches in winter, and cricket in the summer, and Mother could go to concerts and picture galleries. Now my Aunt Madge was getting on in life she must be lonely living in that house in Victoria all by herself. We could join forces with her, as paying guests, of course, and it would help her out.

'You know what it is,' I said to Mother one evening. 'Father will have to think of retiring soon, and what bothers me is how you're going to keep up this house when he does. Florence will have to go, and I shall be out all day at some job typing my poor old fingers to the bone, and here the pair of you will be stuck without anything to do except take Prince for a walk.'

Prince was the dog, and he was getting old like Father.

'Well, I don't know,' said Mother. 'Your father's not due for retirement yet. There's time enough to plan in a year or two.'

'I only hope somebody else doesn't plan for him,' I told her. 'I wouldn't trust that Betty Something-or-other at the office – she has far too much say in things, if you ask me.'

Actually, Father had been looking tired the last few months, and I was not very happy about his health. I taxed him with it the very next day. 'Are you feeling all right, Father?' I asked.

'Yes,' he said. 'Why?'

'You look as if you've lost weight this winter,' I said, 'and you've gone such a bad colour, too.'

I remember he went and looked at himself in the mirror.

'Yes,' he said, 'I am thinner. It hadn't struck me.'

'It's worried me for some time,' I told him. 'I think you ought to see a doctor. You get a pain sometimes, don't you, just under the heart?'

'I thought that was indigestion,' he said.

'Could be,' I said doubtfully, 'but when a man's getting on you never know.'

Anyway, Father went and had a checkup, and although there was nothing radically wrong there was a suspicion of ulcer, the doctor said, and his blood pressure was high. If he hadn't gone for the checkup it might never have been discovered. It upset Father quite a bit, and Mother too, and I explained to Father that it really wasn't fair on Mother to continue working as he did, or on himself. One of these days he would get really ill and have a heart attack in the office, and heaven knew where it would end. Also, cancer doesn't show in the early stages, I told him, and there was no guarantee that he mightn't be suffering from that too.

Meanwhile, I went up to London to see Aunt Madge, and there she was still living all by herself in that house near Westminster Cathedral.

'Aren't you afraid of burglars?' I asked.

She told me she had never given them a thought. I looked astonished.

'Then it's time you did,' I said. 'The things one reads in the papers every day scare me stiff. It's always elderly women living on their own in big old-fashioned houses who get attacked. I hope you keep the chain on the door and never answer the bell after dark.'

She admitted there had been a burglary in a neighbouring street.

'There you are,' I said. 'The brutes are going to start on this district. If you took paying guests, and had a man in the house, nothing would happen. Besides, living alone like this, you might fall and break a leg. Nobody would find you for days.'

I suppose it took me about three months to make the poor dears realise – Father, Mother, and Aunt Madge – how much happier they would be if they pooled their resources and all lived together in the house in Victoria. It was much the best thing for Father, because it meant that he was near to the best hospitals if his health cracked up. It did, too, the following year, but not before I had found myself a job as understudy in a West End theatre.

Oh yes, I was stage-struck, I admit it. You remember Vernon Miles, the matinee idol before the war? He was the heart throb of my generation, like the pop singers for the teen-agers today, and I was mad about him like everyone else. The family were settling in with my Aunt Madge in Victoria – I had the two top rooms as a flat – and I used to go and wait outside the stage door every evening. In the end he had to notice me. My hair was blonde and fluffy in those days, not touched up as it is to-day, and I was really pretty, though I say it myself. Wet or fine, every evening I was there, and gradually it became a sort of joke with him. He started off by signing my autograph book, then he used to say good night and wave, and finally he asked me into the dressing-room for a drink with the rest of the company.

'Meet Old Faithful,' he said – he had a great sense of humour – and they all laughed and shook hands with me, and I told him there and then that I wanted a job.

'You mean you want to act?' he asked.

'I don't mind what I do,' I said, 'as long as I'm inside a theatre. I'll help pull the curtain up and down, if you like.'

I think the audacity of this really did the trick, and the way I wouldn't take no for an answer, because Vernon

Miles did make a job for me as assistant to the assistant stage manager. Actually, I was a sort of glorified messenger girl, but it was a foot on the ladder all the same. And what it was to be able to go back to the house in Victoria and tell them I'd got a job on the stage with Vernon Miles!

Besides the stage directing part of my work, I understudied the understudies. Happy, carefree days they were. The best part, though, was seeing Vernon Miles every day. I was always one of the last out of the theatre and managed to leave at the same time as he did.

He stopped calling me 'Old Faithful' and nicknamed me 'Fidelity' instead, which was more complimentary, and I made it my business to keep away from the stage door all the fans who wanted to pester him. I did the same for other members of the company, and some of them got very jealous. There can be quite a lot of ill-feeling backstage one way or another, which the stars themselves don't see.

'I wouldn't like to be you,' I said to Vernon Miles one night.

'Why not?' he asked.

'You'd be surprised,' I told him, 'the things some of them say behind your back. They flatter you to your face, but it's a different thing when you're looking the other way.'

It seemed only fair to put him on his guard. He was such a kind, generous man, I hated to think of him being put upon in any way. He was a bit in love with me, too, though nothing serious. He kissed me under the mistletoe at a Christmas party, and he must have been a bit ashamed of himself the next day, because I remember he slipped out of the theatre without saying good night.

I waited in the passage every evening for a week, but

191

he always managed to have someone with him – until the Saturday, when I knew there was no one in the dressing-room, and I knocked on the door. He looked quite scared when he saw me.

'Hullo, Fido,' he said – it had got to Fido by now – 'I thought you'd gone home.'

'No,' I said, 'I wondered if you wanted anything.'

'That's very sweet of you,' he said. 'No, I don't think I do.'

I just stood there, waiting. If he really felt like kissing me again I didn't mind. It wouldn't be out of his way to drop me in Victoria, either. He lived in Chelsea himself. After waiting a moment or two, I suggested this, and he smiled, in a strained sort of way, and said he was terribly sorry but he was going out to supper at the Savoy, in the opposite direction.

And then he began to cough quite badly, putting his hand to his heart, and said he was afraid he was going to have one of his attacks – he suffered from asthma, you remember – and would I call his dresser, he would know what to do. I was really very alarmed and I called the dresser, who came at once and put me outside the room and said Mr Miles would have to rest about twenty minutes before going to his supper engagement at the Savoy. I think the dresser was jealous of my friendship with Vernon Miles, because after that night he was always on guard by the dressing-room door and was almost offensive when I tried to hang about outside. It was all very petty and silly, and the atmosphere in the theatre became quite different, with people whispering in corners, and not speaking, and looking the other way whenever I appeared.

Anyway, my stage career was cut short, what with Father's

death (he had an exploratory operation for stomach pain, and although they found nothing organically wrong he died under the anaesthetic), and Mother of course was very distressed. She was fond of Father, in spite of all that nagging, and I had to go home for a time to try and keep the peace between her and Aunt Madge.

The authorities ought to do something for elderly people. It's really terrible, I kept telling them both, how there is no sort of provision for those with failing health. Any day, I said, either of them might get the same sort of pain that Father had, and be whisked off to hospital, and perhaps kept there week after week with nothing wrong. There ought to be hostels, with hot and cold in every room, and a restaurant, and a staff of nurses, so that elderly people could relax and not be worrying about themselves all the time. Naturally I didn't grudge giving up my stage career to look after them, but where would the money come from to keep Mother when Aunt Madge had gone?

Well, that was 1939, and the pair of them were nervous enough then, so you can imagine what it was like when war broke out and the bomb scare started. 'They'll go for Victoria first,' I said, 'because of the station,' and in next to no time I had both of them packed off to Devonshire. But the terrible thing was that the boardinghouse they were staying in at Exeter received a direct hit. They were killed instantly, and the house in Victoria was never so much as scratched. That's life, isn't it? Or perhaps death, to put it correctly.

I was so shocked by the tragedy of poor Mother and Aunt Madge being wiped out by a single bomb that I had a nervous breakdown, and that was really how I came to miss being called up when they started putting girls and young women in the Services. I wasn't fit for nursing, either. I took a job as secretary to a dear old blind million-aire, to try and get my strength back. He had a huge house in Shropshire, and you'd hardly believe it, but, although he became devoted to me, he died without leaving me a penny.

His son came into the place, and his wife didn't like me, or rather I didn't like her, so, as the war in Europe was over, I decided to go back to London, and I got another secretarial job with a journalist in Fleet Street.

It was while I was working for him that I made contact with various reporters and other newspaper people. If you're mixed up in that world you can't help hearing a lot of gossip, and so on, however discreet you are − and no one can call me indiscreet. Scrupulous as you may be, there are limits to what one person can do to quash scandal, and it wasn't my business, even if I'd had the time, to track down every story to its source and find out whether it was true or not. The best I could do, with all the rumours that I heard, was to insist that they *were* rumours and mustn't on any account be passed on.

It was when I was working for the journalist that I met Kenneth. He was the other half of Rosanke. Everyone knows Rosanke, the dress designer and *haut couturier* − whatever you care to call it. I suppose they rank about third in the top ten. People think to this day that it's run by one person, a sort of recluse, shut away in an ivory tower, but the truth is that Rosanke is, or was, Rose and Kenneth Sawbones. The way they put the names together was rather clever, don't you think?

Rose and Kenneth Sawbones were brother and sister, and I married Kenneth. I admit that Rose was the artistic one of the pair. She did the designing, and in fact all the creative work, and Kenneth ran the financial side of the business. My journalist boss had a small interest in Rosanke, just a few shares, but still it paid him to get Rosanke into the gossip columns, which he did very effectively. People were sick of the uniform fashions of wartime, and Rose was clever the way she laid such stress on femininity, hips and bosoms, and so on, and clinging lines. Rosanke went to the top in next to no time, but there is no doubt that it was helped by the push it got from the press.

I met Kenneth at one of their dress shows – I was using a press ticket, of course. He was pointed out to me by a journalist friend.

'There's the *ke* in Rosanke,' said my friend, 'and he holds the tail end, and no mistake. Rose is the brains. Kenny just tots up the figures, then hands in the cheques to his sister.'

Kenneth was good-looking. The Jack Buchanan type, or perhaps you'd call it Rex Harrison. Tall and fair, with bags of charm. The first thing I asked was whether he was married, but my journalist friend told me he hadn't been caught yet. He introduced me to Kenneth, and to Rose too – they were not a scrap alike, although they were brother and sister – and I told Rose what my boss planned to say about them in his paper. Naturally she was delighted, and I had an invitation to a party she was giving. One thing led to another. Rosanke was definitely in the news and getting bigger publicity every day.

'If you smile on the press, the press smiles on you,' I said to Kenneth, 'and once they're on your side the world's your oyster.'

This was at a tiny party I was giving for them, on the

understanding that Vernon Miles would be there to meet them. I'd told them how well I knew him, and they hoped to dress his next play. Unfortunately he never turned up – another attack of asthma, his secretary said.

'What a go-ahead girl you are,' said Kenneth. 'I've never met anyone like you.' And he finished off his fifth martini. He drank too much, even then.

'I'll tell you another thing,' I said. 'You've got to stop letting your sister push you around. Rosanke's pronounced all wrong. You want the accent on the *ke*.'

He sobered up at that. He lowered his glass and stared at me.

'What makes you say that?' he asked.

I shrugged my shoulders. 'I hate to see a man kowtow to a woman. Especially when the man has the brains. It's laziness, that's all. One of these days you'll find the *ke* dropped out of Rosanke, and you'll only have yourself to blame.'

Believe it or not, he took me out to dinner, and I heard the whole story of his childhood and how Rose and his mother had always preyed on him. They were devoted, of course, but, as I pointed out, the very devotion was the worst part about it. It had turned possessive.

'What you need,' I told him, 'is to stand on your own and beat the big drum.'

The result of that dinner was rather extraordinary. Kenneth had a big row with Rose. It was the first they had ever had, he told me afterwards, but it must have cleared the air, because things were on another footing inside the business from that time, and Rose realised that she hadn't got it all her own way. Some of the model girls said that the atmosphere had changed and was spoilt; but that was just because discipline was tightened up and they had to work longer hours.

Kenneth proposed to me in a traffic jam. He was driving me home after a party – I still had the house in Victoria, Aunt Madge had left it to me in her will. We came to a block where the lights had stuck. There must have been something wrong with them.

'Red for danger,' said Kenneth. 'That's you.'

'You flatter me,' I told him. 'I've never thought of myself as a *femme fatale*.'

'I don't know about *fatale*,' said Kenneth, 'but here we are stuck, which is pretty much the same thing.'

Of course he had to kiss me – there was nothing else he could do. Then somebody must have cleared the lights from a main switch. I saw them first.

'You know what green stands for, don't you?' I asked him.

'Yes,' he answered, 'all clear. Go ahead.'

'Well, I'm not married either,' I said. 'The way's clear.'

To be perfectly honest, I'm not certain that he wasn't the teeniest bit taken by surprise. You know how cautious some men are, and maybe he wanted another day or two to bring himself to the point. However, of course word got round in no time that we were engaged, and once that kind of thing creeps into the papers it's so difficult to deny. As I told him, it makes a man look a cad and it's very bad for his business. Besides, it gives people all sorts of ideas when a dress designer is a bachelor. So we were married, and I had a lovely dress on the firm. The only unromantic thing about the wedding was having to become Mrs Sawbones.

Kenneth and I were very much in love, but I had an

uneasy feeling, right from the start, that the marriage wasn't going to work out. For one thing, he was so terribly restless, always wanting to move on from one place to another. We had flown to Paris after the wedding, intending to stay put, but when we'd been there a day he said, 'Dilly, I can't stand this. Let's try Rome.' So off we had to go, there and then, and we hadn't been in Rome two days before he suggested Naples. Then he had the wild idea of wiring for Rose and his mother to come out and join us. On the honeymoon! Naturally I was hurt, and I told him that if it got into the press that he'd had to take his family on his honeymoon, Rosanke would be the laughingstock of London. I suppose that shook him, because he didn't suggest it again. But we didn't stay in Italy long, because the rich food disagreed with him.

Married life . . . what I could say about it, from within! I don't suppose I remember one night, during the six years we were together, that Kenneth didn't have too much to drink. He got so that he couldn't stand and he couldn't speak. He had to go off on a cure three times, but they never did any good. He would seem quite all right in the Home – he tried a different one each time – and then, as soon as he got back to me, off he would be on the bottle again. What I suffered!

No, it didn't make much difference to the business of Rosanke, because once Kenneth started drinking Rose dropped him from the partnership and put a paid accountant in his place. She made Kenneth an allowance – she had to – but it wasn't safe to let him have anything to do with the finances.

I had given up my job, naturally, when I married, but with Kenneth always in and out of nursing homes I had to do something towards expenses, so I kept in touch with my friends in Fleet Street. Nothing official. Just snippets now and again. It helped, being sister-in-law to Rose. You wouldn't believe how much goes on in the fashion world. The buyers hear a lot of backstairs talk, and the model girls too. If customers only realised that every little slip of the tongue gets repeated, they'd cover their lips with sticking plaster every time they went near a fashion house. Anyway, I knew several of the buyers, and most of Rosanke's model girls too. Rose herself wasn't particularly discreet when she was discussing customers inside the family, so I heard a number of stories one way and another that afterwards broke in the press and made headlines. I can't bear gossip, but whispers have a knack of coming true. What's wish fulfilment today is fact to-morrow.

'I think you're a saint,' my friends would say, 'keeping up a home for Kenneth Sawbones, when he's an alcoholic. Why don't you divorce him?'

'He's my husband,' I told them, 'and I love him.'

I believe I could have kept Kenneth off the bottle if only we had had a family. It was not for want of trying, heaven knows. Each time he returned from the Home I would do my best. But it never worked out . . .

Finally, and this was the heartbreak of the whole tragedy, he wrote from the nursing home he had gone to for a fourth cure – away up in Yorkshire it was, too far for me to go and see him on a day trip – and said he loved one of the nurses there, and she was pregnant already, and would I divorce him?

I went straight away to Rose and his mother with the news, and they said they were not surprised. They had felt something of the sort was bound to happen in the end.

They said Kenneth was not responsible for his actions and it was very sad, but the best thing for all concerned was to let him go.

'How am I going to live?' I said. I was nearly out of my mind, as you can imagine. 'Six years I've been a slave to Kenneth, and this is his return for all I've done.'

'We know, Dilly,' said Rose. 'It's been hard on you, but then it's a hard world. Of course, Kenneth will have to pay you an allowance, and I'll look after you too.'

She couldn't afford to quarrel with me, you see. I knew too much about her private affairs and the affairs of Rosanke.

'Very well,' I said, wiping my eyes, 'I'll put a brave face on it, but it comes heavy to get all the kicks in life and none of the sweets.'

There was Rose, rich and famous, fêted by everyone, and I was only Dilly Sawbones, who had helped to put her and Kenneth on the map. It was a hard world, as she said, but she seemed to ride on top of it all right. A penthouse in Mayfair, and lovers by the score, that's what came through being the first half of Rosanke. The second half, or what was left of it, had to make do with a few shabby rooms in Victoria.

Naturally I didn't see so much of Rose once my divorce came through, though she kept her word and made me a titbit of an allowance, enough to redecorate my poor old house. I always got my clothes free, too. After all, everyone knew I'd been married to Kenneth and he had treated me shamefully, and it wouldn't have done the name of Rosanke any good if I'd gone about in rags.

She had a bad streak in her, though, just like Kenneth, and these things always come out in the end. Although I was careful never to say anything against her, she began to lose popularity about that time – there were a fair number of digs at her in the press – and word got about that the fashion house of Rosanke was not what it had been, that it had had its day.

Of course I had to find myself a job. Rose's allowance and the alimony from Kenneth weren't enough to keep me, so I pulled a few strings, and the next thing I knew I was working for the Conservative party before the General Election. I doubt whether the member for South Finchley would ever have got in but for me. You see, I knew a thing or two about his opponent. He used to go about with one of the models from Rosanke, and if there is one thing South Finchley hates, it's promiscuity in a member. I felt it my duty to drop a hint here and there, and our man got in with a slight majority. I'm a great patriot, and I put Queen and country before sentiment or any kind of personal considerations.

Anyway, working hard at the Conservative office helped me to get over losing Kenneth, and it was at one of their meetings that I met Lord Chichester.

'Who's that stiff-looking man with the eyeglass?' I asked someone. I was told at once he was Edward Fairleigh-Gore, whose father had just died, which meant that he had gone to the Lords.

'One of our ablest executives,' said my informant. 'In the running for Prime Minister if the rest of the Cabinet die.'

I managed to get on the fringe of the group surrounding Lord Chichester and was introduced to his wife, a grey-haired woman who looked several years older than he did. It seemed that she was very fond of hunting, never out

201

of the saddle if she could help it, so I asked her what on earth she did about clothes when she came to London, and wasn't it a nightmare wondering if she looked right. Lady Chichester seemed rather surprised, and admitted that the dress she was wearing was two years old.

'You ought to go to Rosanke,' I told her. 'She's my sister-in-law. You need never worry again, once you're in her hands.'

'I don't think I do worry,' said Lady Chichester.

'What about your husband?' I said, and raised my eyebrows. I didn't emphasise the point, and moved out of the group soon afterwards, but what I had said must have made an impression, for I saw Lady Chichester glance in the mirror once or twice, which, without wanting to be unkind, was probably a thing she didn't often do.

The upshot was that I got Rose to send her a card for her next show. The fish were biting that spring, and Lady Chichester went. I was there. I sat beside her and advised her what to order, as she had no sort of taste herself.

I telephoned her every day for a fortnight after that, and finally she invited me to lunch. Lord Chichester came in late, and I only got a word with him when we had coffee afterwards in the drawing-room, but I made myself felt.

'Did you see the bit about you in last night's *Courier*?' I asked him.

'I can't say I have,' he said. 'I never read gossip.'

'This wasn't gossip,' I told him. 'This was the truth, or, if you prefer it, prophecy. "There's only one man who can make the Conservative party into a Fighting Force, and that's Lord Chichester."'

It's a funny thing, but even the most intelligent men

fall for praise. It doesn't matter how thick you lay it on, they revel in it. Lord Chichester smiled and made a sort of brushing gesture with his hand, to pretend it was all nonsense, but I pulled the clipping out of my bag and gave it to him.

That was the start of our affair. It took him over a year to admit that he was lost without me, and when he did he broke down and cried, but then he was not very fit just then and had only recently got over a bad attack of shingles.

'What you need,' I told him, 'is feeding up.'

He was at my house in Victoria at the time. Lady Chichester had broken her leg in a fall out hunting and was laid up in Warwickshire, so Edward – we were Edward and Dilly by then – was on his own in their London house. I was worried that he wasn't feeding himself properly, and it was the worst possible thing for his digestion, as I told him, not to eat, especially after shingles. So one day I waited for him in a taxi outside the Lords and insisted on taking him home so that I could cook him a decent meal. And that was how he came to spend the first night in my house.

'Now, don't worry,' I told him next morning. 'No one will ever find out what's happened. It's between you and me. Of course, if those sharks in the press should get hold of a story it's all U.P. with your career,' I went on with a laugh. I've never seen a man look so frightened – but then, a sense of humour was never his strong suit.

Poor darling Edward . . . Looking back on those years we had together, I realise that I was the great love of his life. I persuaded him that being married to Mary Chichester was no life for a politician; he might as well be married to a horse.

'It's not fair on you,' I said, 'all that stable talk. It won't help you to be Prime Minister.'

'I don't know that I want to be Prime Minister,' he said. 'Sometimes all I feel like is going down to Warwickshire to die.'

'You'll have to take me with you if you do,' I said.

I don't know how it was, but he never seemed to pull his weight in the Conservative party as he should have done. He reminded me at times of Father in the old Eastbourne days. He looked hag-ridden, and when I tried to make him talk about what went on behind the scenes in the House of Lords – because, of course, I still kept contact with my friends in the Press and supplied them with news from time to time – he would try to change the subject and talk about his wife's horses instead.

'You ought to see Ginger,' he would say. 'She's a wonderful mare. And Mary has the lightest hands of any woman I've ever known.'

'The trouble with you is that you've no ambition,' I told him. I couldn't help being bitter at times. There I was, cooking delicious suppers, putting myself out to look after him, and all he could do was to complain of indigestion and rave about his wife's horses.

I never said a word against his wife. After all, she had the money, and it was only a matter of time before she would break her back out hunting, and then darling Edward would be free. It worried me that he made such a fetish of Warwickshire, neglecting his work in the Lords.

'You ought to get the farmers to build their fences higher,' I would tell him. 'If your wife's horses are as good as you make out, they'd leap a haystack.'

And then I'd try to change the subject, get away from

Warwickshire, and put out a feeler or two about his brother peers, or better still the real bigwigs in the Cabinet. It seemed such a waste to have Edward coming round to see me, when it would help him so much to discuss foreign policy and what the Government intended to do about the Middle East, if his brain was going to soften, as it looked like doing. A word or two from me in the right quarter, and the political repercussions might be staggering.

'If you'd only met me ten years ago,' I used to say to him, 'the pair of us wouldn't be sitting here now.'

'You're dead right,' he agreed. 'I'd be in the South Sea Islands.'

He liked to pretend, you see, that all he wanted really was a quiet life.

'No,' I told him, 'you'd be Prime Minister. And I'd be entertaining at Number 10. It makes my blood boil when I see how you let the others pick all the plum positions. You want someone to stick up for you, and the person who ought to do it spends her time gossiping with a lot of grooms.'

I really began to wonder whether the future of the United Kingdom would be safe in his hands after all. There were one or two Labour men who looked as if they had more backbone, and they had more money too. I never had a penny out of Edward – not that I'd have taken anything if he had offered it to me – but I did get rather tired of the framed photographs of horses which he sent me from Warwickshire every Christmas.

No, love stories don't have a happy ending. Not in real life. Mine finished with a bang, and when I say bang, I mean it.

The crisis came when Parliament dissolved at the end

of the summer recess, and I was waiting as usual in a taxi in Parliament Square to pick up Edward and take him home. That was another thing – he was getting so absent-minded that sometimes he went straight home to his own house unless I caught him first. To my horror, I saw him come out of the Lords and make a dive into a car that was drawn up alongside the pavement. The car shot off before I could take its number or tell the taxi to follow it. There was a woman in the back of the car – I could see her through the window.

Here we are, I said to myself. This is it! I went straight back home and put through a call to his wife in Warwickshire. It was only fair to tell her the truth, and that her husband was going out with another woman.

But do you know what happened? The servant who answered the telephone said that Lady Chichester had sold the house in Warwickshire and was up in London, and that she and Lord Chichester were going to Kenya for six months, perhaps a year. In fact, it was very possible that they were going to settle in Africa altogether. Lord Chichester was tired of political life, and he and Lady Chichester both wanted to shoot big game. As far as the servant knew, they were leaving at once, perhaps that very night.

I tried his London house. No reply. I tried every hotel I could think of, without result. I tried the airport and drew a similar blank.

Then it all came out. Lord and Lady Chichester had left for Kenya under assumed names. I read the whole thing in the morning paper. The reason given was that Lord Chichester had had another attack of shingles and wanted to get away from it all. Poor darling – I suppose he was drugged. Handcuffed, even. These things can happen to-day, in a free country. It's a fearful reflection on the Conservative party, and at the next election I'm going to work for Labour. They at least are honest.

Meanwhile, here I am on my own again, with a broken heart. I did everything for Edward Chichester, just as I did for Kenneth, and what did I get out of it? Nothing but ingratitude. I don't suppose I shall ever hear from him again – she'll see to that. If I do, it'll be a buffalo's head on a Christmas card, instead of a chestnut mare.

What I want to know is this: where have I gone wrong in life? Why is it that no matter how kind I am to people, how truly generous, it never seems to pay dividends? From start to finish I've put myself last and the happiness of others first. And yet, when I sit alone now, in the evenings, I seem to see faces around me, Father, Mother, Aunt Madge, Kenneth, Edward, even poor Vemon Miles, and their expressions aren't kind at all but somehow hunted. It's as if they want to be rid of me. They can't bear to be shadows. They'd like to get out of my memory and my life. Or is it that I want to be rid of them? I really don't know. It's too much of a muddle.

My doctor says I live on my nerves, and he's given me a bottle of sleeping pills. I keep them by my bed. But, do you know, I have the impression that he's more worn out than I am. Yesterday, when I telephoned for another appointment, the voice at the other end said, 'I'm sorry, Doctor Yardley is on holiday.' But it wasn't true. I recognised his voice. He was disguising it.

Why am I so unlucky and so unhappy?

What is it that I do?

Note on the Text

With the exception of 'The Limpet', the stories in this collection were written very early in Daphne du Maurier's career, from 1926-1932, although some weren't published until years later.

'East Wind' was first published in the American edition of *The Rebecca Notebook* in 1980, but it can be found in du Maurier's 1926 notebook in the archives at Exeter University. It was not included in the UK edition of *The Rebecca Notebook*.

'The Doll' was first published in *The Editor Regrets*, a collection of short stories edited by George Joseph, published by Michael Joseph in 1937. Du Maurier refers to the story in her memoir *Myself When Young*, which dates it as having been written in 1928.

'And Now to God the Father' was the first story of du Maurier's to be published. It was featured in the *Bystander* magazine in May 1929, just after her twenty-second birthday. The *Bystander* also published 'A Difference of Temperament' the following month.

'And His Letters Grew Colder' was first published in the USA in *Hearst's International Combined with Cosmopolitan* in September 1931.

'The Happy Valley' was first published in the *Illustrated London News* in 1932.

'Frustration', 'Piccadilly', 'Tame Cat', 'Maizie', 'Nothing

Hurts for Long' and 'Week-End' are from *Early Stories*, published in Great Britain by Todd in 1955. The stories in this collection were all first published in journals and magazines between the years of 1927-30.

'The Limpet' appeared in the American edition of *The Breaking Point*, published by Doubleday and Co. in 1959. It was not included in the UK edition.